THE HAREM

A STEAMY ADVENTURE

VICTORIA RUSH

VOLUME 30

JADE'S EROTIC ADVENTURES - BOOK 30

COPYRIGHT

The Harem © 2020 Victoria Rush

Cover Design © 2020 PhotoMaras

All Rights Reserved

FEEL THE RUSH:

Jade's Erotic Adventures – Book 1

When lonely divorcée Jade seeks to broaden her horizons, she's invited to a private dinner event which promises to stimulate all of her senses. Wearing nothing but masquerade masks, dinner guests receive special service under the table while their fellow diners look on...

The Dinner Party

Jade's Erotic Adventures - Book 2

Jade discovers an exotic adventure club where strangers meet to explore each other's bodies in mysterious dark rooms. Using special effects to project swirling light patterns onto their figures, the shifting shadows provide just enough illumination to highlight their naked bodies while protecting their identities...

The Dark Room

Jade's Erotic Adventures - Book 3

Jade discovers a yoga club where members stretch and explore each other's bodies in the buff. She books an appointment, and during the first session meets a young redhead who tantalizes her with her flexibility and stunning body...

Naked Yoga

For the uninhibited...

SPICY ADVANCE EXCERPT:

I turned around and saw Fatima smiling at me in the soft moonlight, and she leaned in to kiss me. Whether she was trying to express her gratitude for my helping to save her or she was just curious about feeling my fair skin, I couldn't be sure. But either way, I was happy to accommodate her newfound intimate interest in me. As we began to kiss more passionately, intertwining our tongues and pressing our bodies together, she pulled my robe up over my hips, caressing the outside of my thighs and my round buttocks.

But when her hand curved around to my bald pubis, she gasped and uttered something in arabic. I heard Laila reply to her in the darkness on my other side, and Fatima giggled as Laila rolled over to sandwich me between the two of them. Suddenly I had two pairs of hands caressing my body from both sides, and I moaned as they slipped their fingers between my thighs, caressing my vulva from two ends. I pulled Fatima's smock higher, feeling her fluffy bush caressing my bare mound, and I groaned in her mouth as her fingers found my pleasure spot and she began rubbing my clit in soft circular motions. But when I felt Laila's fingers press inside my slit and begin finger-fucking me from behind, I began rocking my hips, moaning more loudly.

When the rest of the girls began to realize what the three of us were up to, it didn't take long for the entire group to devolve into a moaning, slithering mass of naked bodies writhing under the thick jumble of cotton robes and woolen blankets. I pulled Fatima's dress all the way over her shoulders and squeezed her bare tits while she played with my clit and moaned into my mouth. It didn't take long for the combined action of her manipulation of my clit and Laila's caressing of my vulva to bring me to the brink of pleasure. As the two women pressed their bodies tightly against mine, I felt my orgasm overtake me and I jerked my body spastically, gushing all over the two girl's hands...

1

———

As I walked through the open-air market in Marrakesh, I could feel my heart pounding in my chest. I'd never been to Morocco before, and the hustle and bustle of the *Souk Semmarine* was a feast for the senses. With so many tourists and locals crammed into the narrow laneways, my eyes darted from one distraction to another. While I strolled past their stalls, shopkeepers noisily hawked their wares, begging me to make an offer on everything from cheap jewelry to handbags. The pungent aroma of grilled kebabs, fresh hummus, and fried snails permeated my nose. Everywhere I looked, women in long, full-body burkas or face-concealing niqabs passed calmly by, seemingly unperturbed by the chaos of the teeming bazaar. With my long blonde hair and tight jeans, I definitely stood out like a sore thumb in this conservative muslim metropolis.

After a half hour or so, I grew tired of the peddlers confronting me, and I ducked into one of the shops to try on some head scarves, hoping to distract attention from my obvious Western appearance. When I tried a pretty pink and teal colored one on and looked at myself in the tiny mirror on the wall, the owner came up behind me, smiling at my reflection.

"Very pretty," he said. "You like?"

"Maybe," I said, mindful of the hard-sell personality of local merchants that I'd been forewarned about. "How much is it?"

"For you, pretty lady, only five hundred dirham!"

Knowing the local exchange rate was roughly ten dirham for one U.S. dollar, fifty bucks for a scarf didn't seem out of line. But I also knew that shop owners in North African bazaars were notorious for fleecing unaware tourists and that haggling was an expected and necessary condition of purchase.

"That's more than I can afford," I said, placing the garment back on the rack.

"Perhaps we can make an accommodation," he said, lifting the scarf off the shelf and placing it back on my head. "Since the colors match your eyes so perfectly."

"Um-hmm," I smiled, knowing full well he was just buttering me up for a sale.

"How about two-fifty?" I said, placing my hands on my hips defiantly.

"Ps-shaw!" the merchant scoffed. "That is well below my cost. This is an authentic Moroccan hijab. Other merchants sell this style for much more."

"Well, I guess I'll just have to go check *them* out then," I said, placing the scarf in his hands and turning to exit the stall.

"Ok, ok!" he backpedaled, catching up with me and blocking my exit. "New price, only for you. Four-fifty. But that's as low as I can go."

"That's not much of a discount," I huffed. "Other vendors have offered far better. Three hundred is the best I can do."

The man threw up his hands, wrinkling his brow with a sad puppy dog face.

"My lady, I wish I could help you, but I'm just a poor merchant with high overhead. Don't you expect me to make a profit?"

"Of course," I said. "But I know most of these items have a high markup. I think you've still got plenty of profit to work with here. Perhaps I'll come back after comparing prices with some of the other sellers."

"Wait, wait," the man said, stepping in front of me again. "I can't have you leave without purchasing something. Four hundred is my best offer. But at that price, you're practically *stealing* it from me."

I picked up the scarf again, turning it over to look for some kind of label.

"How do I know this is even made here? There's no tag."

"Oh please," the man said, crossing his arms. "Now you *insult* me. We only sell authentic textiles manufactured in this country. Look at the intricate stitching. This is hand-embroidered right here in Morocco."

"And the fabric?" I said, rolling the cloth between my fingers. "Is it genuine silk?"

The man placed the garment under an overhead ceiling light, slowly tilting it from side to side.

"Can't you see how the patina changes color when you bend the fabric? I would never sell cheap polyester at my store. This is where all the local muslim women come to purchase authentic Arab clothing."

"Okay," I said, shaking my head in surrender. "I'll offer a little more since I can tell it's a quality product. "I will pay three hundred and fifty dirham, cash. That is all I have on my person."

The merchant paused for a moment, scanning my face with a stern expression as if trying to divine my thoughts. Then he burst into a broad smile, nodding enthusiastically.

"Only for you, my pretty American," he said. "And only because I don't want to see you walking around the bazaar in a cheap knock-off sold by the other vendors."

"Good," I said, turning back toward the mirror. "Do you mind showing me the proper way to wear it? The way the local women do?"

"Of course," he said, draping the scarf over the top of my head and pulling the ends softly under my chin, tying them in a gentle knot. "The idea is to cover your hair and tie it so it covers as much of your face as possible. Our culture requires women to express their modesty by covering their bodies when they are out in public."

"Thank you," I said, pulling some bills out of my pocket and handing him the agreed-upon amount.

"Please, come again," the man said, bowing with his palms centered over his chest. "I have many more items of clothing that you would look beautiful in."

"I'll try to come back before I leave your beautiful country," I nodded. "Thank you for your time."

"Safe travels," he said, waving goodbye to me as I exited the stall.

While I continued down the main thoroughfare jostled by distracted tourists, aggressive shopkeepers, and beguiling snake charmers, I realized the thin head covering provided limited camouflage from my fair skin and Western clothing. By the time I exited the packed marketplace, I was visibly sweating and exhausted. I found a nearby cafe and ordered a strong coffee, then found a vacant table in the corner and sat down, nursing my drink.

Most of the patrons appeared to be Westerners, but on the far side of the room sat a lone man in long white robes wearing a traditional headdress, sipping a beverage. I'd always been fascinated by the clothing and customs of native Arabs, and as he appraised the boisterous tourists gathering in the cafe, he peered at them bemused. The man had dark, weathered skin and a closely cropped beard with soft brown eyes and a square jawline. Appearing to be in his late thirties or early forties, he was quite handsome, with the juxtaposition of his flowing cream-colored kaftan and his golden-brown skin making him look like a young Omar Sharif.

As he casually glanced around the cafe, he caught me staring at him, and I quickly looked away. Moments later, my gaze was drawn back to him and this time he smiled when our eyes met. When I looked away again, he stood up from his table and went to the front counter where he placed an order for something. A few minutes later, the clerk handed him two steaming cups and the man began walking in my direction.

"Excuse me," he said, approaching my table. "I noticed you were sitting alone and wondered if you'd like some company. I brought you a cup of mint tea if you'd like to sample some of our local fare."

"Um..." I hesitated, looking around the room to make sure it was safe to be seen in the company of a stranger.

Normally, I'd quickly rebuff someone who made such a bold and unsolicited advance, but there was something about his quiet demeanor and warm eyes that put me at ease.

"Thank you," I said, shifting my chair back a few inches. "That would be lovely."

"My name's Amir," he said, handing me the cup of steaming tea.

"Jade," I said, nodding politely toward him.

"That's a lovely name. It sounds Asian or Moorish, but you look much *fairer* than that."

"Yes," I laughed. "I suppose my light skin gives me away. I'm from Chicago actually, in the United States."

"I know it well," he nodded. "The Sears Tower, Navy Pier, Millennium Park..."

"You've *been* to the United States?" I said, surprised by his fluent English and knowledge of my local landmarks.

"I spent four years studying law at Columbia University and traveled throughout the country during my summers off."

"I *wondered* where your perfect English came from," I said, smiling at his handsome face. "I never would have guessed–"

"That a sheep-herder like me might be so worldly?" he joked.

"No," I stammered. "I meant–"

"It's okay," he laughed. "It's a common reaction I get from Westerners. They either expect me to be some kind of sultan or a terrorist wearing these clothes."

"I'd never judge a person simply on the basis of what they're wearing," I said, furrowing my brow in sympathy.

"That's very wise," he said, peering up at my scarf. "What about you? You seem to be a little more...*restrained* compared to your fellow countrymen."

I lifted my hand self-consciously to my scarf and chuckled.

"I felt a little exposed walking around the markets with

my long blonde hair. I think I was too easy a mark for your local merchants."

The man took a sip of his tea and chuckled.

"They can be a little overbearing at times when it comes to approaching tourists. There's something to be said for exercising a little decorum and good manners."

"I couldn't agree more," I said, lifting my cup in agreement.

"So, what brings you so far from home?"

"Just looking for a change of pace, I guess. I've never been to this part of the world and I wanted to experience the unique culture of North Africa."

"Where have you been so far?"

"Just the medina and a few of the museums. But I'd love to see more of the countryside."

"You mean the *desert*? There's really only two climate zones in the Mediterranean crescent–the fertile orchards near the sea and the barren plains of the Sahara."

"I guess I'm more drawn to the desert. Maybe it's from watching all those romantic films like Lawrence of Arabia and The Wind and the Lion. There's something about the natural beauty of the red sand and the windswept dunes that seems so peaceful and alluring. It seems to be about as far away from the hustle and bustle of the urban jungle as you could possibly get."

"Have you ever ridden a camel?"

"It's on my bucket list."

"Would you like to join my caravan for a little excursion?"

"Caravan?" I said, widening my eyes. "You're traveling in a *caravan*?"

"Yes," he nodded. "It's a modest group. A few camels, some livestock, and my small coterie."

"Is that how you get around?" I asked, suddenly intrigued by this mysterious stranger. "Where are you from originally?"

"I was born in Jordan, but I come from a Bedouin family. We're nomads, moving from country to country, buying and selling livestock and living off the land."

"So you really are a–"

"Goat herder?" he laughed. "In a manner of speaking. But as the leader of my tribe, I'm officially considered a *sheikh*."

"But what about Columbia...?"

"My wealthy parents sent me there hoping for bigger things for me. But I prefer this simple life. There's something to be said for the freedom and stress-free life of a traveling vagabond. I get to meet interesting people in all the countries along the North African peninsula."

"Just like Sean Connery in the movie The Wind and the Lion," I smiled.

"I suppose, insofar as being the king of my domain and living a nomadic lifestyle. So what do you say? Do you feel as brave as Candice Bergen?"

"As I recall, she didn't exactly go *willingly* into the Sahara wilderness with her would-be captor. And I don't have any romantic intentions..."

"No worries," the man said. "You can stay as long or as short as you prefer, or even just for a day trip through the edge of the desert on one of my camels. I assure you that I have plenty of *other* distractions at my disposal."

I pinched my eyebrows, appraising the mysterious man in luxurious robes. I had no doubt that he had little trouble attracting beautiful women wherever he traveled.

"How would this work exactly?" I said, crossing my arms. "I've never run off with a strange man into the desert before."

"I understand your hesitation," he said. "My camp is just

outside the city limits. You can join my troupe for an authentic Bedouin dinner while you stay with my other wives in a separate tent. If you feel so-inclined, you're free to join us on the next leg of our journey toward Algiers. I'll be happy to pay for your safe passage back to Morocco if that's where you've made return travel arrangements."

I paused for a moment, scanning his face for any sign of ill intent. I'd heard about the legal practice of polygamy in certain Arab countries, and far from turning me off, the idea of being surrounded by other women who could satisfy his sexual needs gave me a certain degree of comfort.

"That won't be necessary," I said. "It shouldn't be too difficult to change my airfare if necessary. But how can I be sure you don't intend to steal me away like Sean Connery and add me to your stable of harem girls?"

"That's not the way we operate," he laughed. "As you probably learned from watching that movie. Honor is the most important character trait among we Bedouin. But of course, I would encourage you to leave a message with your friends and family before you leave."

The man took a menu scrap from the table and scribbled something on the paper.

"This is my full name. I'm well known in most towns along the coast. The last thing I need is the American cavalry hunting me down like in the movie. I assure you, this is an honorable offer between friends. You have my word on that."

"Can you give me a day to think it over?" I asked, still not convinced this was a good idea. But the lure of joining a real caravan through the Sahara Desert was awfully tempting.

"Absolutely," Amir said. "If you decide to join me, let's meet in this cafe at the same time tomorrow. If you're not here, I'll understand and there will be no hard feelings. But if you do decide to come, we can take a taxi to the outskirts of the city where my aide will meet us and escort us by camel to my camp at the edge of the desert."

"How will I keep from falling off?" I smiled.

"It's not as scary as it looks to ride a camel," he said. "There are comfortable and secure saddles, and they walk quite slowly. But if you're still worried, you can always ride tandem with me."

"I'm sure I'll be fine," I smiled, turning my wrist to check the time. "Thank you for your kind offer, Amir. I look forward to meeting you again tomorrow at five p.m. And thank you for the tea."

As I rose to leave, he stood along with me, extending his hand.

"I hope to see you again, lovely Jade," he said, clasping my hand softly. "And keep an eye out for those carnival barkers. Best to keep your hijab on while you're walking about town."

"Will do," I said, heading toward the exit door.

After I left the cafe, I closed my eyes, inhaling the warm arid air of the Moroccan town square. Something told me that my North African adventure was about to take an interesting new turn.

2

For the next twenty-four hours, I vacillated back and forth on whether to entertain the handsome sheikh's offer. On the one hand, I'd always dreamed about trekking through the Sahara Desert on a camel. But I knew that traveling into the wilderness with a total stranger was not without its risks. He could easily abduct or molest me, with no guarantee that the local police would make any effort to find me or hold him to account. I knew that muslim law was highly skewed in favor of the man's rights and that women were often ostracized or worse for any kind of perceived sexual indiscretion.

The following morning after enjoying a light breakfast, I approached the front desk of my riad to enquire about the mysterious man. If he was as important and well-traveled as he claimed to be, I figured the staff of one of the best hotels in Marrakesh would have heard of him. But if he was an unknown or persona non grata, I'd simply ignore his invitation and remain in the relative safety of the downtown tourist areas.

"Excuse me," I said, slipping Amir's handwritten note

across the counter towards the attending clerk. "Can you tell me if you've heard of this man?"

The clerk squinted at the writing then looked up at me and smiled.

"Of course," he said. "Mr. Haddad is one of our frequent guests. Would you like me to see if he's staying at the hotel?"

"Um, no, thank you," I said. "It's just that he invited me to take a tour with his caravan and I wondered if this was, you know–*safe* or irregular."

"I can't vouch for how often he entertains Westerners in his cavalcade, but he is often seen in the company of attractive young women such as yourself, and I've never heard of any complaints or misconduct. The Sheikh is widely respected as a man of honor and prestige in these parts. I'm quite sure that you would not only be safe, but indeed well-protected while under his guardianship."

"Thank you," I said, placing the note back in my pocket.

As the hour approached for our planned reconnection, I packed a light duffel bag of overnight clothes and sent an email to my best friend Hannah from back home.

Han,

Enjoying my trip to Morocco so far. Will send more pics soon. I've accepted an invitation to go on a private caravan tour of the local desert with a prominent bedouin leader. His name is Amir Haddad. Apparently his family is quite prominent in Jordan.

If you don't hear back from me in a few days, contact the local embassy to see if they can track my whereabouts. I know this sounds crazy, but I've always dreamed of traveling the Sahara on camelback, and you only live once!

Talk soon,

Jade

I knotted my silk scarf under my chin, then placed a wide-brimmed straw hat on my head and headed back towards the cafe where I'd met the sheikh the previous day. With my heart beating a million miles an hour, I strolled past the bustling souks wondering what I'd gotten myself into.

When I entered the cafe and saw Amir sitting in the corner with his legs crossed sipping a cup of tea, he smiled and stood as I approached his table.

"I'm glad you decided to join me again, Jade," he said, holding out his hand as he supported me while I lowered myself onto the adjoining chair. "I was afraid that I might have scared you away with my rather direct proposition."

"I went back and forth considering it, to be honest," I said. "But I asked around, and you were truthful about your reputation. Apparently, I'm not the *first* tourist you've entertained in this manner. But I left your credentials with the U.S. Embassy just in case."

"I would expect no less from such a wise and pretty lady," he smiled. "May I order you a cup of tea?"

I looked at my watch and glanced outside at the lengthening afternoon shadows.

"I'm already pretty charged up about this adventure," I said, concerned about traveling at night deep into the outback. "Shouldn't we head out to your camp while there's still good light?"

"As you wish," he said, standing up and extending his hand as he surveyed my wardrobe. "I see you've come well prepared for the elements. Though I'm not sure about that

hat. You look more like *Audrey Hepburn* in Breakfast at Tiffany's than Candice Bergen in The Wind and the Lion."

I smiled at his genteel manners while he opened the cafe exit door for me then hailed a passing taxi. After we got in the cab and he gave the driver directions in arabic, he glanced down at my overnight bag.

"It looks like you're intending to stay for a while," he smiled. "I must not have scared you *too* much with my abrupt proposition."

"I've heard it's a pretty big desert," I said, pulling my handbag closer toward me. Unbeknownst to my host, I'd included a can of pepper spray under my belongings in case he got the wrong idea. "A girl can never be too prepared on these kinds of expeditions."

"Indeed it is," he smiled. "Did you know that the entirety of the Sahara Desert is even bigger than the continental United States? But never fear—my caravan has enough provisions to keep us comfortable for as long as you choose to stay."

As the taxi sped towards the outskirts of the city, I watched the passing scenery as it became progressively less populated and more barren. Within twenty minutes, the dusty streets soon gave way to grassy hillsides. When we crested the final ridge and I saw the open expanse of the desert stretching out in every direction, I gasped. The late afternoon sun cast long shadows over the undulating red sand dunes, making it look like a different *planet.*

"Is this your first time seeing the desert?" Amir asked, noticing my wide eyes surveying the eerie landscape.

"First time up close and for *real,*" I nodded in a daze. "It's even more magnificent than I imagined."

"It has a way of transporting you," he nodded. "There's something about the open vistas and the way the sun reflects over the shifting sands that's quite captivating. Perhaps now you can begin to appreciate how I'm are attracted by its allure."

"It *is* mesmerizing, I grant you," I said. "But how do you navigate your way across this moonscape? There are no roads or landmarks to know which way you're headed?"

"We navigate by the shadows of the sun during the day and the stars in the evening. Plus, the desert isn't all sand. There are bluffs and oases and mountain ridges that point our way. We bedouin have traveled the deserts of North Africa for thousands of years. We know it as well as the back of our hands, as you Americans say."

"I'll have to take your word for it," I said, suddenly feeling the dryness in my mouth. "But something tells me I should have packed more bottles of water in my overnight case. How far away is your camp?"

"It's only twenty or thirty minutes by camel ride," Amir said as the taxi skidded to a stop at the end of the road. Nestled in a shaded dale of the hillside, I noticed a dark-skinned Arab man in a long tunic tending to three camels. "My aide brought an extra ride for you. Don't worry about the water. We've long-since learned how to manage our scarce resources in the parched desert."

Amir paid the taxi driver then escorted me to the dale where he introduced me to his servant.

"This is Ali," Amir said, motioning toward the other man. "He'll look after all of your needs during your stay with us."

The man bowed slightly at the waist, acknowledging me as Amir's guest. I found it a bit strange that Amir didn't introduce me by name, but I assumed it had something to do with the customs of his tribe and his status as leader of the clan.

I glanced at the three oddly shaped animals nibbling on grass besides us. With their long knobby legs, U-shaped neck, and large hump in the middle of their back, they looked like a cross between a llama and an oversized donkey. Towering at least two feet over the top of my head, I was already starting to get vertigo imagining myself trying to balance on top of their precarious mounds.

"These are a lot *taller* than I imagined," I said, noticing an absence of stirrups hanging from their woven cloth saddles. "How will I ever get on top of it?"

"You don't climb up on a camel like you would a horse," Amir said. "They kneel down for you to get on top of them."

He mentioned something to his aide in arabic and Ali pulled on the long hair on the side of one of the camels, then the animal knelt down on the ground with its front knees and lowered its back end until its belly was lying flat on the ground.

"Wow," I said. "That's certainly convenient. Have you trained them this way only for your guests, or is this the way *everybody* mounts a camel?"

"They're very domesticated," Amir said. "It's easy enough to climb atop a standing camel if you know how, but this certainly makes it a lot easier."

"I'll say," I nodded, seeing the top of the cloth saddle now resting at hip height.

"But you still need to be careful to hold on to the pommel at the front of the camel's saddle to make sure you don't get bucked off when it stands. It jerks forward and back as it rises, and if you're not used to it, you can easily be thrown."

Amir said something to Ali and he held out his hand, motioning for me to climb atop the saddle of the resting camel, and I swung my leg up over his hump and sat down on the surprisingly comfortable seat. Although the frame appeared to be made entirely of wood, I noticed a padding of straw and palm leaves under the thick woven blankets draped over its flanks.

"Okay," Amir said. "Now grasp the knob on the front of the saddle tightly and clamp your legs against the side of the camel as he rises."

I did as Amir instructed, then Ali tapped the side of the animal and it lurched forward lifting its back end, then it stepped forward with both front legs until it was fully erect. My body swung wildly as it see-sawed up to a standing position, and I could feel my heart beating as I stared down at the ground ten feet below me.

"Are you good?" Amir called up to me, seeing the fright in my eyes.

"Yes, as long as I don't fall off," I grunted. "But how do I *steer* this thing?"

"Don't worry about that," he laughed. "Ali will lead your camel with a tether behind his animal. But watch out as he begins to walk. They have a bit of a jerky gait. Try to relax your body and let it sway with the animal's movements. Are you ready to head out to our camp?"

I nodded my head then Amir and Ali mounted their camels, heading out in a straight line toward the open desert with Amir in the lead. It didn't take long for me to get used to my camel's rhythmic up-and-down gait, and as I began to relax, I looked out over the vast expanse of russet-colored dunes at the exquisite beauty of the desert. Looking like a giant Rothko painting, all I could see was an endless sea of golden waves juxtaposed against the brilliant blue sky.

The air was hot and dry, and I blinked as sprinkles of sand dusted up into my eyes from the strong wind sweeping across the dunes. More than once I had to grab my hat from falling off my head from the gusts shooting overtop the crescent-shaped hillocks. As I watched the long shadows of our three camels traipse across the soft turf, I smiled at the serene beauty and solitude of the glittering landscape. I wasn't sure what awaited me at Amir's camp, but for the time being, the gentle loping of my camel and the whisper of the warm Saharan breeze lulled me into a blissful, trance-like state.

3

———

Thirty minutes later, I noticed a clump of trees on the horizon, and I squinted through the shimmering haze wondering if it was a mirage. But as we got closer, I saw a small collection of tents nestled among the palms and a flock of livestock grazing on the grass surrounding the perimeter of the encampment. Hardly believing my eyes, I called ahead to Amir, wondering how anything could grow in this barren wasteland.

"Is this your camp?" I shouted over the howling wind.

"Yes," he said, pulling his camel up beside mine so I could hear him better.

"I thought my eyes were playing tricks on me at first," I said, shaking my head in astonishment. "How does any vegetation survive out here without any water?"

"The desert is riddled with a labyrinth of underground aquifers," he said. "In certain places, natural springs bring the water to the surface, feeding the surrounding vegetation. At other oases, manmade wells tap the aquifers, supplying much needed water to traveling caravans such as my own."

"I thought oases were just a figment of Western movies I

had no idea they actually existed in the middle of the desert."

"There are actually quite a few scattered across the Sahara," he nodded. "But because of the vast size of the desert, it can take many days on camel to travel between them. They've been the lifeblood of we bedouin for centuries."

As we got closer to the camp, I noticed a large herd of camels and scores of sheep and goats grazing quietly in the grass.

"And there's enough water to feed all those *animals* too?"

"Yes," Amir said. "The aquifers are practically endless. There's a veritable ocean of water underneath this arid surface. Did you know that the Sahara was once an enormous sea before the Earth's shifting plates separated the large continents of Eurasia and Africa?"

"I had no idea," I said, growing increasingly impressed with Amir's knowledge of world history and geology. "But why do you have so many camels and livestock? You must have quite a large entourage."

"Actually, it's mostly just me and Ali and my stable of wives. The animals are primarily used to transport our gear and provide food for our band."

"Wow, you really *are* a self-contained entity out here in the middle of the wilderness, aren't you?"

"Everything we need is supplied by the animals and the desert," he nodded.

"And your *wives*," I smiled, peering ahead toward Ali plodding along in front of us, wondering how he satisfied some of *his* more primal needs.

"Yes," Amir smiled. "And my wives."

When we reached the edge of the trees, I noticed a group of women kneeling in the sand preparing food. They all wore loose-fitting tunics and cotton headdresses that wrapped tightly around their heads and faces, providing protection from the overhead sun and the dusty wind. As our retinue approached the center of the camp, the women looked up and stared at me like I was from another planet. They all seemed young and strikingly beautiful.

Maybe Amir doesn't need to entertain Western women after all, I thought.

The two men dismounted their camels, then Amir tapped my animal and he knelt onto the ground, where Amir offered his hand to help me dismount. Then he led me into one of the two large tents in the campground where an attractive dark-haired woman roughly my age was folding clothes in the corner of the enclosure.

"This is my wife, Laila," he said, introducing me to the woman. "Laila, Jade will be joining us for dinner this evening, so please make sure she has everything she needs."

She turned around and smiled at me with her piercing eyes. I was surprised how beautiful she looked bereft of any makeup or other embellishments. Her wraparound head-dress framed her pretty face, highlighting her high cheek-bones and golden-brown skin.

"Pleased to meet you," Laila said, bowing slightly at the waist.

It was hard to discern her figure under her layered cloak, but my pussy fluttered when I saw her face flush slightly in modesty.

"You speak *English*?" I said, surprised by her absence of any discernible accent.

"Yes," she said. "My family is from Cairo and we learned English in elementary school. I'm a bit rusty, so it will be nice to have a native speaker to help me brush up on my skills."

"We'll be having dinner when the sun goes down," Amir interrupted. "Then I'll be providing some special entertainment in my tent later on. You may wish to put on some warmer clothes, as it can get quite chilly outside after dark. I'll see you in another hour or so."

After Amir exited the tent, I peered at Laila with a quizzical look.

"*Entertainment*?"

"Never fear," she chuckled. "He often entertains visitors with a traditional arab dance. Though it's usually for the benefit of other men. This is the first time he's brought a Western *woman* into his camp."

"I guess I should be honored then," I shrugged, wondering exactly what kind of dance he had in mind.

Laila peered at my cut-off capri pants and light linen blouse and smiled.

"Would you like to change into something more comfortable? As Amir said, it gets quite cold at night and you'll want a bit more protection against the blowing wind."

"Sure," I said, happy to adopt the local customs during my brief visit with the group.

"If you'd like to remove your clothing, I can store them in a safe location while you stay with us."

"*Everything*?" I said, wondering what arab men and women wore underneath their long garments.

"It's more comfortable that way," she said. "Unless you need to wear something because it's that time of the month...?"

"No, thankfully," I chuckled, curious how they also managed *that* aspect of their personal hygiene.

As I began to remove my clothing, Laila peered at me, noticing the strange tan lines around my bra and upper arms. I paused for a moment before pulling off my panties, and her eyes widened when she saw my shaved pubis. I felt like a bit of a freak, realizing that she and the rest of the women rarely went outside with any exposed skin and almost certainly abstained from any kind of intimate grooming.

Laila fetched a neatly folded garment from the corner of the tent then opened it up to reveal an ankle-length tunic with long sleeves and an opening at the top. I held up my arms and she draped it over my body, stepping in close to me as she peered into my eyes. She smelled of jasmine and lemongrass, and my heart fluttered as her full lips neared my mouth when the garment fell over my shoulders. Then she wrapped a long cotton scarf over my head and under my chin, fastening it with a bobby pin at the ends to hold it in place.

I guess they're not completely bereft of Western conveniences, I smiled.

When she finished, she stepped back and nodded approvingly, smiling at the unusual appearance of a Western woman dressed in traditional arabian garb.

"Do you have a mirror or something to view myself in?" I asked, intrigued to see what I looked like.

"I'm afraid we don't," she said. "It is not part of our culture for women to primp over their external appearance. But I assure you that you look quite beautiful."

"Thank you," I said, reaching into my bag to retrieve my phone. I tapped the screen a few times then handed the device to Laila. "I know this must sound terribly touristy of me, but would you mind taking a picture of me? My friends back home will never believe that I got myself into this arrangement, and I'd love to have a keepsake of my visit to your camp."

"Okay," Laila said, squinting her eyes at the phone. "But

this is a little different from the phones I remember using in my youth. How does it work?"

"Just step back and angle the phone until you see my entire body on the screen, then tap the red button at the bottom to capture the image."

Laila did as I requested and I heard the familiar shutter sound when the phone took the picture. She handed it back to me and I tapped the thumbnail image in the lower corner of the screen to view the full-size image. I laughed when I saw myself encased in the flowing robes, with only my pale face peering through the wraparound fabric.

"That's certainly a different look for me," I said, feeling the soft fabric brushing against my hardening nipples and bare mound. "But I have to admit, it's a lot more comfortable than my usual attire. Is it comfortable to wear in the heat of the day?"

Laila pulled the fabric up over my shoulders and I felt a puff of air press up from the floor toward my exposed pussy.

"The cotton fabric breathes nicely, and the loose fit permits the wind to flow over our bare bodies underneath," Laila smiled.

"Yes, I can see that," I said. "I'm *already* beginning to appreciate the extra freedom of movement in this dress. Although I don't imagine you call it that in your native language."

"We women refer to it as a *thawb*, but when men wear similar robes, they call it a kaftan."

I nodded, beginning to understand the various ways arab culture subjugated women under the control of men. I crossed my arms, beginning to feel the chill as the sun began to set over the horizon.

"Do you think this will this be warm enough in the evening?"

Laila pulled a wool blanket off the pile of clothes in the corner and placed it over my shoulders.

"This shawl will help keep you warm," she smiled. "And it can also be used as a bed covering later on at night."

"Speaking of," I said. "I see you don't have any traditional beds in the tent..."

"We bedouin can't afford such luxuries," Laila laughed. "Everything has to be light enough to pack onto the backs of our camels when we move from one location to the next. We sleep on woven blankets on the soft sand. I think you'll find it's quite comfortable, actually."

"Does everyone sleep in this one tent?" I said, peering at the limited amount of floor space in the twenty-by-twenty-foot enclosure.

"All of the *women*, yes," Laila nodded. "The men have separate tents, of course. Everything is tightly controlled in our caravan. Nothing goes to waste."

"So I'm beginning to learn," I smiled, imagining myself lying on the soft desert sand next to the covey of beautiful women at night.

"Are you hungry?" she asked.

The mention of food made my stomach grumble. I suddenly realized that I hadn't eaten since early in the morning.

"Oh yes, very."

"Come, let's show you how we prepare our traditional bedouin meals."

Laila led me outside, where a large open fire cackled in a sand pit with a wooden frame erected overtop of its perimeter. The women sat in a large circle around the flame, hunched over in their long robes, kneading their hands into large porcelain bowls.

"It smells heavenly," I said, breathing in the fresh scent of milk and spices. "May I ask what the women are preparing?"

"It's a rice dish infused with fresh goat milk, lentils, and chopped onions, seasoned with saffron and turmeric."

"So you're all *vegetarians*?"

"Oh no," Laila said. "We also eat goat meat and lamb. But that's usually reserved for special occasions, like when we have a guest such as yourself."

"I see," I said, noticing Amir flipping open the canvas door of his tent and walking in our direction.

"I see that Laila has gotten you into some more comfortable clothes," he nodded approvingly. "Are you ready to enjoy our traditional bedouin dinner?"

"Absolutely," I said. "I don't know if it's this desert heat or the long camel ride, but I'm famished!"

"Well, we won't delay any longer then," he said, brandishing a curved knife from under his kaftan. He walked up to one of the younger sheep grazing quietly at the edge of the pasture and he grabbed the animal by the back of its head, calmly slicing its throat. The lamb staggered for a moment in shock, then fell to the ground twitching its legs for a few seconds, then lay still as the blood from its neck coated the desert sand. Seconds later, Ali approached the dead animal, and using a longer knife proceeded to slice open its belly, pulling out its entrails.

"Oh my God," I dry-heaved, turning away from the scene of the gory slaughter.

"You've never seen a live animal killed before?" Amir said, seeing my discomfort.

"Never up close and in person like this," I coughed, trying to keep myself from retching.

"But you eat meat?"

"Yes, it's just that–"

"You Westerners are insulated by your supermarkets and hidden slaughterhouses from the act of killing and preparing the animal."

"Yes," I said, realizing how hypocritical it was of me to be offended by the practice of killing live animals for consumption.

"A halal slaughter is considered the most humane way of killing an animal in our culture," he said. "The animal hardly feels a thing before it loses consciousness and quickly bleeds out."

"I'll take your word for it," I said, watching Ali skin the animal and thread a stake through its mouth as he placed it over the fire pit.

"I hope this won't diminish your appetite for the meal. Everything should be ready in another half hour or so."

"I'm sure I'll be fine," I said, smelling the scent of the fresh meat cooking over the pit. "I just need a moment to collect myself."

"Come join me then by the fire while the women make the final preparations."

Amir motioned to a blanket spread out on the sand about ten feet away from the fire, and he held my hand while I sat down on the mat.

"So, what do you think of our little caravan so far?" he said, sitting down cross-legged beside me.

"It's certainly *authentic*," I said, peering at the group of young women preparing the dishes in the circle around the fire. "But I'm wondering about the ratio of men to women in your troupe. Are all of these women your wives?"

"Not in the *legal* sense," he said. "I prefer to think of them as my courtesans."

"They're all so young and pretty. How did they come to join your caravan?"

"I bought them," Amir said nonchalantly.

"You *what*?"

"I know this is a custom frowned upon in the West. But it is quite common in conservative muslim cultures, especially among we bedouin. Families consider it an honor for their daughters to be indentured to a prominent sheikh such as myself."

"And when they get *older*? Do you simply dispose of them when they no longer suit your fancy?"

"They're sold off to other prominent men as maids, nannies, and cooks. The women are always treated well, generally enjoying lives far more comfortable and secure than in their own impoverished families."

"And in the meantime, they travel in your caravan for your own amusement?"

"Well, as you can see, they perform many *other* useful functions. Nobody goes for want in my troupe. Everyone's needs are fully satisfied."

"What about *Ali's* needs?" I said, noticing his servant dutifully turning the roast lamb on the fire spit. "Does he also enjoy the company of these attractive ladies?"

"He would never dare *touch* one of my women for fear of instant execution," Amir said, suddenly clenching his jaw. "But he's well compensated for his service to the caravan. He satisfies his more primal needs in the many small towns along our route."

"I see," I said, watching him remove the charred carcass from the spit then carving it up into smaller chunks and passing them around the circle. Each of the women took a piece and sliced it up into bite-sized portions, mixing them in with their bowls of rice.

"Come," Amir said, taking two bowls and placing them in front of us. "Let's not be concerned about such indelicate matters over dinner. Let's enjoy our feast under the stars of this magnificent canopy."

He picked up his bowl and dipped his hand into the dish, pinching skewers of meat and rice between his fingers and bringing it to his mouth. Looking around the circle, I saw the rest of the entourage doing the same, and I picked up my bowl not wanting to be rude, following their lead. The food was surprisingly moist and tender, with the milk-infused rice keeping all the ingredients bound together, making it easier to take bite-sized chunks in my fingers. I hummed appreciatively at the piquant taste of the freshly prepared ingredients, soon forgetting about the unsettling scene that I'd witnessed with the young lamb moments before.

As we all ate quietly around the circle, my eyes scanned the faces of the pretty young women peering at me curiously across the dancing flames of the bonfire. It didn't take long for my mind to wander to what *other* forms of entertainment they used to keep themselves amused when Amir was otherwise occupied. Surely, he couldn't keep *all* of them satisfied at one time, I thought. As my pussy twitched from the cool desert breeze wafting up under my fluttering robe, I began to look forward to sleeping on the soft desert sand later in the evening.

4

After dinner, Amir invited Laila and me to his tent to enjoy the planned entertainment. He motioned for two of the girls to prepare for the event, and they left the circle while the rest of the women cleaned up the dishes. When I entered his enclosure, I was surprised at how large it was for one person. More than twice the size of the women's shelter, it was bedecked with persian rugs, beautiful tapestries, and a large wood-frame bed with luxury linens.

Wow, I thought, shaking my head in dismay. *Arab men really do enjoy all the advantages in this culture.*

Amir invited the two of us to sit on the plush carpet in the center of the tent, then he fetched a heart-shaped guitar from the corner and sat down between us with the instrument cradled between his legs. A few moments later, I heard two women's voices outside the front door of his tent and Amir replied to them in arabic. When they pulled back the flap and entered the room, my eyes flew open in shock. Instead of their usual long robes and wraparound headdresses, they wore a skimpy ornamental bikini costume

Their long black hair was held in place by a beaded headband with long tassels hanging down over their eyes, festooned with little silver bells. Dangling from their tasseled bikini bottom hung a knee-length black cloth that provided a modicum of modesty to cover their crotch area. But the rest of the costume left little to the imagination, showing the deep cleavage between their tightly compressed breasts and their exposed bellies and thighs glistening in the soft candlelight of Amir's tent.

Shifting from the ultra-conservative full-body covering of their traditional frocks to this bawdy costume was a shock to my system, and I soaked up the women's taut, sexy figures like I hadn't seen a near-naked body in weeks. Which I damn near *hadn't*. Suddenly realizing that I hadn't felt the touch of another woman's body since I left home, my pussy throbbed while I ogled the sexy girls standing only a few feet in front of me.

"Are you ready to watch a real arabian belly dance?" Amir said, noticing my pupils dilated in excitement.

"Definitely," I smiled, eager to see the two women gyrate their bodies next to me.

He nodded toward the two girls and they stepped back a few feet, then he picked up the guitar and began strumming a rhythmic folk tune. As the melody filled the cabin, the two women began to undulate their hips in unison, matching the beat of the song. My eyes flickered over their bodies, absorbing the sensuous spectacle while their stomach muscles flexed and their navels swayed from side to side like two winking eyes. As they stepped forward and back in perfect harmony, they snapped the castanets on the tips of their fingers together, providing a rhythmic accompaniment to Amir's lilting melody.

Just when I thought this guy couldn't get any more suave and sophisticated, I thought. *He even plays the guitar perfectly.*

In another place and time, I might have fallen for his seductive demeanor, but for the time being I was utterly hypnotized by the sensual moves of the two beautiful women dancing before me. As I watched their eyes gazing at us behind their swinging ringlets, I tried to place how old they were. Their bodies hardly had an ounce of fat, and their skin was as soft and supple as a teenager's. Knowing many arab countries had few restrictions against marrying much younger women, I wondered if they were even of legal age. As if that actually mattered out here in the middle of the desert.

Amir softened the strumming of his guitar and the girls eventually slowed their movement to a stop, then he turned toward me and smiled.

"What do you think of our traditional arab music and dance?" he said to me.

"It's beautiful," I said, shifting my position on the warm carpet, suddenly realizing how wet I'd become watching the two girls. "And very sensuous."

"Yes, it is," he said. "Do you have a particular request?"

I shook my head, unsure what he meant at first, then I cleared my throat when I realized he was talking about the music and not what I wanted to do with the girls.

"You mean like a Western *song*?"

"Yes," he nodded. "I always like to satisfy my guests' preferences."

I thought for a moment about a song that resonated with me that was also slow enough to fit with the girls' style of performance.

"Do you know the Bob Marley song Waiting in Vain, but played in the style of Annie Lennox?"

"Of course," he said. "It's one of my favorites."

He began strumming his guitar again, and the familiar melody of the song filled the tent while the two girls swayed their hips in harmony with the rhythm, clapping their castanets softly to provide gentle background accompaniment. A few moments later, Laila began humming the tune and Amir turned toward her, encouraging her to join him.

From the very first time I laid my eyes on you, girl, she sang with an angelic voice. *My heart said follow through. But I know, now, that I'm way down on your line...*

I turned to face her, amazed that she knew the lyrics to the song and enthralled by her gorgeous tone.

But the waiting feeling's fine, she cooed, meeting my gaze. *So don't treat me like a puppet on a string. 'Cause I know how to do my thing...*

Suddenly my thoughts echoed back to earlier in the day when she slipped my robe over my naked body, and the way she peered at me as she leaned in toward me.

Had she felt the same sexual attraction I'd had for her when we first met?

As she sang the words, she looked into my eyes and smiled while I tapped my feet rhythmically against the soft carpet.

I don't want to wait in vain for your love, she sang, gazing at me directly as my mouth parted in a spellbinding stupor. Suddenly, I couldn't wait to get out of Amir's tent and back into the women's enclosure where I could lie next to her on the warm desert sand under my soft wool cape.

As the song wound down and the girls' movement slowed to a stop, Amir placed his guitar to one side and reached around behind him, placing two odd-looking drums on the mat in front of him. Made of different-sized hollowed-out ceramic bowls with dried animal skins stretched over top, they looked like homemade bongo drums. As if on cue, Laila reached beside her and picked up a wooden reed instrument fashioned in the manner of a flared flute.

"That was beautiful," I said, peering at the two of them. "I don't think I've enjoyed that song as much as I did just now. This whole experience has been a feast for the senses."

Amir smiled as he pulled the drums in closer toward his knees.

"I'd like to finish with song I wrote myself for this kind of occasion," he said. "Unfortunately, I can't sing as well as Laila and her mouth will be otherwise occupied during this tune, so you'll just have to enjoy the *other* elements of the performance," he said, nodding toward the two belly dancers.

As he began beating on the drums with two hands, Laila picked up the flute-shaped instrument and began humming another arabic tune, tapping her fingers rhythmically over the holes on top of the shaft. The girls began swinging their hips slowly at first, but as Amir began increasing the pace of his tapping, they gyrated their hips faster and faster, turning their bodies around as I watched their buttock muscles flexing and shaking under the silk tassels hanging down from their tight bikini bottoms. As Laila matched Amir's escalating backbeat in pace and volume, the girls grew increasingly animated with the shaking of their bodies, looking like they were building up to some kind of climax.

While they shook their bodies with increasing passion and fervor in the form of a simulated sex act, I found myself shifting my weight again on the warm carpet underneath me, growing progressively wetter from their suggestive body movements and facial expressions. Amir became increasingly energetic pounding his drums with his two hands, and

I noticed that he was staring at the girls with a lustful look in his eyes. The sexual tension in the room was now at a fever pitch, and as he banged out the last part of the performance, I saw a light sweat dripping over his brow. When he finished the song with two loud bangs on the drums, for a few moments everything in the tent became still as I listened to the sound of everyone's heavy breathing.

"Did you enjoy our little performance this evening?" he said, turning to face me after a long pause.

"Yes, very much," I panted, suddenly realizing how much the performance had raised my *own* heartbeat.

"If you'll excuse me now," he said, looking at the two scantily clad girls in front of him and motioning for them to stay behind. "I think it's time for me to turn in now. Laila will look after your sleeping arrangements. I'll see you again in the morning."

"Thank you," I said, as Laila and I stood to leave. "I'm sure I'll sleep very soundly this evening."

When I followed Laila out the front flap of Amir's tent, I noticed a dark shadow moving away from the perimeter and I recognized Ali's shape in the flickering moonlight. I shook my head realizing that he'd been spying on the erotic performance through a hole in the tent and picked up my pace to catch up with Laila.

"It's as simple as *that*, is it?" I said, referring to Amir's unbridled control over the girls. "He only has to nod, and the women submit to whatever his request?"

"Unfortunately, yes," she said, peering at me with sad eyes. "He's bought and paid for us, and we have to do whatever he says."

"Even if that means sleeping with him whenever he demands?"

"*Especially* that," she said.

"You seem somewhat less eager than the other girls," I said.

"He's had his way plenty enough times with me," she shrugged. "Thankfully, he now prefers the younger girls. Did you at least enjoy the performance?"

"Yes," I said. "It was very–*stimulating*. But honestly, I enjoyed your singing more than anything else. You have a gorgeous voice. Even when you played the wind instrument, I couldn't take my eyes off of you."

"Thank you," she said, noticing me pull my wool shawl over my shoulders to protect against the biting desert wind. "You have a very intoxicating manner about you as well. Come, let's get out of this cold desert air and bundled underneath something warmer."

When we entered the women's tent, all the other girls were already lying fast asleep on their blankets on the sand, with only one small open spot left in the corner of the enclosure. Laila laid a large blanket down over the space, then nonchalantly pulled her dress up over her shoulders, folding the robe and headdress on the ground next to the blanket. I couldn't help staring at her voluptuous body, highlighted by the lone flickering candle next to the makeshift bed. Her breasts were full and firm, resting high on her chest with dark medallions encircling her thick, pointed nipples. Her bare hips curved sensuously around the dark patch of pubic hair on her mound, tapering to long but muscular legs. In the dark shadows of the enclosed pavillion, she looked to me like some kind of sexy Amazon.

Then she picked up a large woolen blanket and threw it over her shoulders, lying down on the carpet peering up at me.

"Are you just going to stand there, or are you going to get under the covers and help keep me warm?"

"In the *buff*?" I said, unsure what the proper protocol was for women sleeping together in the tight confines of the communal tent.

"It's more comfortable that way," she said. "The less washing of our clothes that we have to do, the better. We prefer to air them out overnight. Besides, the sheepskin feels so much better against your bare skin. Come join me if you feel brave enough."

I pulled off my shawl and lifted my thawb over my shoulders, placing them gently on the sand on the other side of the blanket, then lifted the fluffy duvet and nestled in next to her.

"Oh, I'm feeling brave enough," I said, turning to face her.

"Good," she said. "Because those dancing girls weren't the *only* thing distracting my attention this evening."

5

———

Laila turned her body toward me, then shifted her weight closer, wrapping her legs around my hips. I could feel her soft bush caressing my bare mound as she pressed her breasts firmly against my chest. I placed my hand against the side of her head and leaned in to kiss her, and our tongues melded together in a different kind of erotic dance.

"Laila," I whispered. "I'm so happy we have a chance to sleep together. I've wanted you from the moment I laid eyes on you."

"Why do you think I joined the two of you in Amir's tent?" she said, smiling into my eyes. "I wanted you all to myself."

"Weren't you worried that I might have stayed with *him* instead?"

"Possibly," she cooed. "He certainly knows how to put on the charm when he wants something."

"I already made it clear to him that I didn't come here for *romantic* reasons," I said. "Besides, men don't really do it for me any longer."

"Oh?" she said. "You prefer the company of women?"

"Only *certain* ones," I purred, grinding my pussy against hers.

"Do you mind if I examine you more closely?" she said. "I've never seen a Western woman up close and naked before. You're very–*different*."

"Absolutely," I said. "I've been fantasizing about you strumming your fingers over something other than that *flute* for the last half hour."

"Mmm," she groaned, moving further under the blanket.

As she nibbled her way down my body, I felt her hard nipples etching a line over my trembling stomach. When her mouth reached my breasts, she circled my teats with her warm tongue then sucked them hard into her mouth as she squeezed my mounds with both hands. Unlike the tender manner of most new lovers, I reveled in her rough and dominant style of lovemaking. If this was the way arab women made love to one another, I was ready to be taken.

I placed my hands on the back of her head and pulled her harder against my chest, burying her face between my cleavage. Then I lifted my right knee and pressed it between her splayed legs until it stopped against her wet vulva. She sighed as I began to rock my hips forward and back, stretching the skin of my thigh over her burning pussy.

"Lick me down below," I panted, rolling my hips frantically against her belly. "I need to feel your hot lips on my pussy before I explode."

"Soon enough," she said, blowing softly on my belly as she inched her way down toward my aching snatch.

But when her face reached my shaved mound she paused, feeling my bare skin while she rolled the sides of her cheeks against my soft flesh, kissing me softly at the apex of my slit where my labia merged together at the top of my clit.

"Oh *God* yes," I panted, feeling her warm lips touching my sensitive organ for the first time. "Lick my slit and taste my juices. See how wet you've made me."

She pressed her head a few inches lower, then ran her flat tongue over the length of my folds, lapping up my dripping juices.

"Yes, I can see that," she purred. "You taste much better than goat's milk over rice."

"Yes," I gasped. "Suck on me like a tender lamb. I want to feel your tongue probing every part of me."

Laila curled her tongue as she mashed her face between my legs, pressing it deep into my hole. I grabbed her head, pulling her harder against my cunt, rubbing her face up and down my dripping crease. There was something about the raw act of fucking her naked on the desert sand that I found incredibly arousing. Seeing her wrapped up in her full body covering and suddenly feeling her naked body writhing next to mine took me to new heights of pleasure.

"Mmm," I groaned. "I need you to suck my button now. I want to feel your tongue on my clit. Suck me, Laila."

"Hmm," she purred, moving her head higher up on my slit.

When she surrounded my jewel with her lips I almost came right away, but she seemed to sense my heightened state of arousal and for a long moment she held her head still between my legs while she felt my clit pulsing in her mouth. But when she began rolling her tongue over my nub in slow sensuous arcs, bathing me with her warm saliva, I couldn't help moaning out loud.

"God, yes," I panted. "That feels so good. I needed this so badly,"

"Mmm-hmm," Laila nodded, feeling my juices running down her chin and neck.

I could feel my passion beginning to rise and I could have come quite easily from the action of her tongue alone on my raging clit, but what she did next took me to an entirely new level of ecstasy. She slipped two fingers of her right hand into my hole and buried them knuckle deep while stretching her little finger further down my perineum and circling it over my tender anus.

Fuck me, I thought. *This girl really knows how to make love to a woman.* I wondered just how much extra-curricular activity went on at night in the privacy of the women's tent while the other men were sleeping. I had no idea, but I was certainly interested in finding out.

When she began curling the two fingers inside me toward my G-spot, I arched my back and began grunting like a wild animal. I couldn't hold back the floodgate of pleasure any longer as my orgasm suddenly overtook me like a freight train.

"Yes, Laila!" I wailed. "I'm going to come, baby. I'm going to come all over your pretty face."

Part of me wanted to warn Laila about my tendency to squirt when I was this wet and worked up, but there wasn't any time. I suddenly felt the muscles of my pussy begin to clench uncontrollably, gushing my pent-up juices all over her slippery face and the soft blanket below us.

"Uhnn," she groaned, seeming to enjoy my orgasm almost as much as I was while she felt the walls of my pussy contracting powerfully on her fingers still deeply embedded inside me.

It must have taken over a full minute for me to stop coming in her arms with the most powerful orgasm I'd had in months. When I finally began to calm down, I collapsed onto the moist blanket and turned to kiss her softly on her lips.

"Thank you," I said, running my fingers through her hair. "I really needed that."

"You seemed to be already pretty worked up. Did you get that excited watching the two girls performing their special dance?"

"I have to admit that I did," I nodded. "I don't know if it was because I was so surprised to see their almost naked figures or because of the way they were moving their bodies, but it didn't just put *Amir* in the mood for some extra night-time fun."

"So you're attracted to women also?"

"Definitely," I said. "I find women are more adept at satisfying my sexual needs, just as you were a few moments ago. In fact, your special expertise suggests this wasn't the first time you've made love to a woman either."

"Of course not," she smiled. "What do you think we girls do with ourselves in this tent when we're left to our own devices?"

"*All* of you?" I asked, feeling my juices dripping out of my slit once again at the thought of the pretty girls having a group orgy in their little pleasure dome.

"Um-hm," Laila nodded. "There are twenty women but only one penis in our traveling caravan. How *else* do you think we satisfy our needs?"

"What about poor Ali?" I said. "Isn't he ever allowed to get in on the action?"

"Amir would never share the women he's bought and paid for with another man. It would be considered a violation punishable by death if he so much as *looked* at one of us the wrong way. Besides, with his hooked nose and foul-smelling breath, none of us would ever be interested in him that way."

"Well I'm certainly interested in *you* that way," I smiled, threading my thigh again between her legs toward her steaming pussy. "It's my turn to give you the kind of pleasure you just administered to me."

As I began to move my body lower under the blanket, Laila suddenly stopped me, flipping me over onto my back.

"Why don't we *both* share the pleasure this time?" she said, rolling her body on top of me and lifting my left leg while she pressed her wet vulva against my pussy.

"If you insist," I said, smiling up at her.

"I want to watch you this time while I make love to you," she said. "I've never made love to a white girl before."

I smiled at her reference to me as a white girl, even though we were both technically caucasian. But there was no denying that she was considerably darker than me, and I felt a similar sexual attraction to her exotic appearance.

"I'm sure it's not so different from the *other* girls you've fucked," I said, feeling her thick bush pressing against my bald pubis. "Other than being *bare* down there."

"Like a little girl," she grunted, beginning to grind her twat against mine.

"Does that turn you on?" I said, reaching up to pinch her thick nipples as her large breasts swayed overtop my chest.

"Maybe," she said. "I've never felt a woman's bare *kus* before."

"Not even when you experimented when you were younger?"

"Never like *this*," she panted, rocking her hips more rapidly against mine as the sound of our wet pussies slapping together filled the cabin.

"Fuck my girly pussy, Laila," I teased her, recognizing that she was getting turned on by the naughty imagery. "I want to gush all over your furry snatch when we come this time."

"Yes," she huffed, throwing her head back in pleasure as we squeezed each other's breasts tightly with both hands. "You're so wet and slippery down there. I like the feeling of your bare sex against me."

"Would you like to try it yourself sometime?" I said, lifting my hand to her face as she sucked my thumb into her mouth. "Perhaps I can groom you myself while I'm here."

"I'm not sure Amir would appreciate me defiling my body in a way that's not in accordance with muslim custom."

"But you already said he rarely shows interest in you that way. This can just be between the two of us. It will grow back within a few weeks after I leave."

"I'm not sure I'm going to *want* you to leave after this," she said, pulling my leg up higher as she wrapped her arms around it, pulling it tightly between her sweating breasts. "Come with me, Jade. I want to feel your juices mingling with mine when you climax this time."

"*Fuck* yes," I panted, just waiting for her signal. "Grind your pussy against mine. I'm going to cum all over your hairy bush. Here it comes, baby."

"Uhnnn!" Laila suddenly grunted, throwing her head back in rapture, and for the second time that evening, I felt my body pushing over the precipice as another powerful orgasm washed over me and I began squirting jets of liquid all over Laila's twitching pussy.

As we watched each other's bodies convulsing atop one another in the dim light of the tent, I suddenly heard the soft squealing sounds of the other women around us while they pleasured themselves listening to the two of us. Something told me my little caravan excursion was about to stretch out into a longer adventure than I'd planned.

The following morning, Laila and I rose at the break of dawn and got dressed, heading outside for breakfast. Amir was already sitting around the fire pit with a scattering of women preparing the meal. He smiled when he recognized me wearing my thawb and invited the two of us to sit beside him.

"Did you sleep well last night?" he asked me.

"Yes, thank you," I said. "I found it surprisingly comfortable sleeping on the desert sand."

"It's fine as long as you have a thick blanket underneath you. The grains have a way of finding their way into every nook and cranny of your body if you're not careful out here. I prefer to sleep a few inches off the surface myself."

I peered around the circle and recognized the two girls from last night's belly dance performance back in their long robes and headdresses, baking flatbread atop a curved metal hotplate.

"That smells wonderful, whatever it is you're making," I said, choosing to ignore his none-too-subtle intimation about our sleeping arrangements.

"Fresh flatbread and yogurt," he said, motioning to the tall trees surrounding the encampment. "With a side portion of dates, harvested directly from these palm trees."

I shook my head in awe at the simplicity of their nomadic lifestyle.

"I'm amazed how self-sufficient you can be simply from what you carry with you across the desert."

"Yes," he nodded. "Our goats provide milk, cheese, and yogurt, and the sheep provide all the meat we need. Everything else is supplied by the markets we visit along the fringe of the desert on our caravan route."

"If you don't mind my asking," I said, watching the women flipping the sizzling flatbread over the metal hotplate. "How do you pay for the extra materials? I mean, how do you earn hard *currency* while traveling across the desert?"

"Primarily from our livestock," Amir said. "Our animals are quite prolific, and there's a strong demand for these animals wherever we go. The camels in particular are very valuable commodities since they live for so long and can travel long distances without any water."

I glanced at the herd of camels grazing on the sparse grass and drinking from a wooden trough next to the well.

"And they're able to carry your entire entourage with all of its regalia across the open desert?"

"Yes, they're very strong and hardy animals. We'd never be able to survive out here in the middle of the desert without them."

The girls placed some of the fresh flatbread on individual plates along with bowls of yoghurt and chopped dates, then passed them around the circle to the now fully assembled group.

"Please—eat up," Amir said. "You'll need your strength if

you plan to stay with us a little longer. The desert provides, but it also takes away. Your body burns a lot more calories in this sweltering heat."

I watched him dip his flatbread into the bowl of yogurt and pick up the dates with his fingers, and I followed his lead. Everything tasted incredibly fresh and delicious and when I finished my plate, I licked my fingers clean like the rest of the group.

"Oh my God," I sighed. "I could get used to this way of life. Everything is so simple and easy out here. Even the food tastes better than what I'm used to at many five-star restaurants. Talk about farm to table!"

"Are you enjoying it enough to *join* us on the next leg of trip to Algiers?" Amir smiled.

I paused for a moment, remembering what I'd told Hannah before I left my hotel in Marrakesh.

"How far away is it? I told my friends they should expect to hear back from me in a few days."

"It six or seven days by camel ride. But we'll be sleeping out in the open most nights under the stars. We only set up camp when we stop near towns or at the few oases along our route."

"I think I can manage that," I nodded, smiling at Laila remembering how much I enjoyed sleeping next to her on the warm sand last night. "But only if you let me help clean and pack up like everyone else. If I'm going to join your troupe for a few days, I want to feel like a productive member of the tribe."

"If that's what you wish," Amir nodded. "Laila and Ali can look after whatever you need. Will you have any trouble making return travel arrangements from Algiers?"

"It shouldn't be a problem," I said. "As long as it has an international airport."

"Indeed it does," he said, standing to leave. "I'm going to collect my things while Ali begins dismantling the tents. We'll be setting out within the next hour."

I was surprised how quickly the group broke down the camp, neatly arranging all the tent poles, coverings, and contents atop the backs of the camels. When we were ready to leave, we filled our saddlebags with enough water to last us for a few days, then we headed east two-abreast atop the remaining camels. It was quite a sight watching the long train of animals traipsing through the pretty sand ripples lining the undulating desert with nothing to keep us occupied but the shifting shadows of the sun and the howling desert wind.

At nighttime, we circled the camels and livestock around us to provide a modicum of cover from the blowing breeze, then laid down on our individual blankets and woolen duvets to keep ourselves warm. I missed sleeping with Laila and more than once thought about sneaking under the covers to join her, but I dared not risk disturbing Amir and Ali who were sleeping nearby.

After three days, we came upon another small oasis and set up the tents once again to provide a respite against the searing overhead sun. I was thrilled to have another chance to make love to Laila in the relative privacy of our own tent, and after the girls fell asleep, she let me shave her mound with the travel razor I'd packed in my bag, using goat's milk and yogurt as an improvised shaving cream. Afterwards, I licked her clean as she knelt over my face writhing in pleasure while I sucked her bare vulva and clit into my mouth.

But the following morning, something happened that forever changed the course of my dreamlike desert adventure. As I flipped open the flap of our tent to fetch some water from the well, I noticed Fatima, one of the girls who'd performed the belly dance a few nights earlier, lifting a pail out of the well while Ali snuck up behind her, trying to lift her robe while he pulled his erect penis out from under his kaftan. When she ducked aside to evade his unwanted advance, he suddenly lost his balance and tumbled head over heels into the well, screaming all the way down until I heard a loud splash when he fell unconscious at the bottom of the pit. Fatima looked around her with frightened eyes and we she saw me watching, she rushed toward me crying, throwing her arms around me wailing in arabic.

Not wanting her to be discovered, I ushered her quickly into our tent and explained to Laila what had happened. A few seconds later, Amir emerged from his tent alarmed by the commotion, calling out Ali's name. Suspicious when he didn't immediately hear his reply, Amir went back into his tent and came out carrying a flashlight, pointing it down into the well. When he saw Ali's body floating face-down in the pool of water, he turned toward our tent and stormed toward it, angrily flipping open the door covering.

He glared at Laila with steely eyes and a red face, speaking loudly to her in arabic. She said something back to him and shrugged her shoulders, feigning ignorance at what had just transpired. He then approached each of the girls separately, asking them if they knew what had happened. But we got to Fatima, he noticed that she was shaking and he placed his hand under her chin, raising her face to meet his angry gaze. She shook her head, afraid to admit any involvement in the incident, but when he saw her dried tear tracks, he grabbed her hair, dragging her outside.

I looked at Laila bewildered and asked what was going on.

"It's not good," she said, following Amir outside. "Just stay close to me and don't say anything."

"Why don't we just tell him the *truth*?" I said. "That it was an innocent mistake, and that she was just trying to protect herself from Ali's unwanted advance?"

"It doesn't work that way," Laila said, shaking her head. "The scales of justice are tipped greatly in favor of the men in our culture. If she were discovered to have been involved in his death, even incidentally, it wouldn't end well for her."

"So what happens if nobody's willing to talk?"

Laila gritted her teeth as she watched Amir remove his long curved knife from under his belt and place it over the fire. I watched the steel grow red-hot in the flame, then he pulled Fatima's head back and placed the hot blade next to her face. He said something angrily to her and she shook her head frighteningly. Then he forced her mouth open as she slowly extended her tongue. He placed the flat side of the knife on it and she screamed as the blade made a horrible sizzling sound against her flesh.

"What the *fuck*..." I said, stepping toward her trying to intercede.

"Don't," Laila said, grabbing my arm.

"But what he's doing to her in *inhuman*," I protested. "She's just an innocent bystander–"

"This is the way justice is administered in the bedouin culture. When there's a dispute involving a serious crime and no one comes forward to admit guilt, the men administer what is called a *bisha'a*, which is a type of trial by ordeal. The accused person is forced to lick a hot piece of metal and if the tongue shows any sign of a burn or a scar, this is considered a sign of guilt."

"Of *course* her tongue will burn!" I exclaimed. "He just placed a red-hot *knife* against her flesh!"

Amir removed the knife from Fatima's mouth, then doused her tongue with a ladle of fresh water. Then he peered closely at it and threw her down on the sand, cursing at her in their native tongue.

"So what happens now?" I said to Laila.

"If a woman is convicted of this type of crime, she's usually sentenced to death, often by public stoning. But Amir won't do it himself. He'll have to take her to a local tribal court where judgement will be formally handed down and administered by the muslim council."

"You've got to be kidding me," I said, hardly believing what I'd just seen and heard.

Amir turned around noticing that Laila and I had witnessed the entire scene, and walked toward us with flaring nostrils.

"I'm sorry you had to see that," he said to me. "But what Fatima did was a serious crime that cannot be ignored. She will have to face the consequences of her actions. Laila, I want you to coordinate with the other women so we can pack up the camp immediately. We'll be heading out to Algiers as soon as possible to have Fatima's fate decided."

"Wait!" I said, stepping toward Amir in desperation. "I saw the whole thing. She didn't do anything wrong. Ali assaulted her and she was simply trying to defend herself. It was just an accident when he tripped and fell into the well."

Amir paused for a moment as his eyes flashed over my beseeching face, then he shook his head dismissively.

"She must have done something to provoke him," he said. "He couldn't have fallen so easily into the well. We will see what the tribal council decides in Algiers."

"And if she's found guilty?" I said.

"She'll be put to death immediately," Amir said, turning to head back to his tent.

I tried to follow after him, but Laila grabbed my robe, holding me back.

"He can't get away with that!" I said, turning toward her. "It's barbaric!"

"Unfortunately, this is the way of our culture. If a muslim woman is even *suspected* of fraternizing inappropriately with a man other than her husband, Sharia law dictates that she be summarily executed."

"By public *stoning*? What about the guilt of the *man*? What if it's simply one person's word over another?"

"In our culture, the man is always presumed innocent since they have free rein over the women and females are instructed to refrain from fraternizing with anyone other than their husbands."

"I'd hardly refer to what they were doing at the well as *fraternizing*. There's only one place for everybody to collect water out here. It's inevitable that there'll be some form of close contact among such a small group in close quarters. Surely something can be done–"

"I'm afraid we have no control over the situation," Laila said, looking at me sadly. "It's out of our hands now."

Later that evening, we stopped in the middle of the desert to rest for the night and grab a bite to eat, and everybody sat around the campfire looking sadly at each other. Nobody dared say a thing, knowing full well what Amir's intentions were. I peered at Fatima, shivering next to the fire as Laila wrapped her arms around her, trying to provide a modicum of comfort. When we dispersed after the meal to make our individual beds in the sand, I took Laila aside and peered into her eyes.

"We can't just let this poor girl be unjustly punished for a crime she didn't commit," I pleaded.

"What would you have us do?" she said. "*He's* the one with all the power and the control. We can't just overpower him and run away."

I crossed my arms and shook my head at the absurdity of the situation.

Laila paused for a long moment, then looked up at me through narrowed eyelids.

"There might be *another* way we can extricate ourselves from this unfortunate situation," she said. "What if we steal away in the middle of the night and take all the camels with us? He won't be able to follow us, and he'll run out of water long before he gets to Algiers."

"But he'd *die* out here in the middle of the desert without any food or water!" I said.

"It's either him or Fatima," she said. "Who do you think is more deserving to live? The innocent girl who did nothing other than try to protect herself from a violent rape, or the man who summarily judges her based on his ludicrous code of honor?"

"But he seemed to be so–"

"Sophisticated, and a man of the world?" Laila said. "There are two sides to every man, and this one is no different. He may have been educated in your country, but I assure you that his morals and underlying character have been indelibly shaped by his family affiliations and the culture of his tribe. Are you prepared to do what has to be done?"

I paused for a moment, trying to think of any other conceivable options, then I grudgingly nodded. I couldn't believe that my exciting desert adventure had suddenly turned into a deadly serious conspiracy where two people's lives lay in the balance.

Laila and I waited until we heard Amir snoring under his blanket, then she roused each of the girls, telling them about our escape plan. Everybody got up and tiptoed through the sand toward the camels, then we tethered them together and mounted them carefully, slowly leading them away from the rest of the livestock herd.

"What about the goats and the sheep?" I whispered into Laila's ear, who I'd paired up with on the lead camel.

"We haven't got time to gather them together and we can't risk disturbing Amir–"

Suddenly I heard a man's voice yelling in the darkness, and I turned to see Amir rising from his sleep and begin chasing after us. Laila kicked the sides of her camel and the whole train burst into a gallop, creating a dusty trail behind us. Amir screamed and shook his fists as he tried to catch up with us, but he was no match for the fleet group of camels, and within seconds he disappeared behind us in the thick cloud of dust.

"*Jesus*," I said to Laila after we'd put a few hundred meters between us. "Are you sure this is going to work? Now we're *all* unwitting accomplices in this sordid affair."

"We're at least three days' camel ride to the nearest village on the outskirts of the desert," she said. "It would take three times as long to cover that distance on foot. There's no way he can survive in this stifling heat for that long without water."

"And the *rest* of the animals?"

"They're a bit more hardy. We can come back for them a little later when the coast is clear."

I peered behind me to see the other girls following behind Laila's camel in single file.

"What will you and the others do now that you're no longer part of Amir's caravan?"

"I plan to send them back home to their families when we get to Algiers. This many camels will fetch more than enough money to arrange safe transit to their home ports."

"What about *you*? Won't people be looking for Amir at some point if he doesn't show up? Surely his family–"

"I plan to be long gone before anyone raises any suspicions. I've got some extended family in the Andalusia region of Spain where I can lay low for a while. I'm more worried about you. Did you tell anyone that you were going to join Amir's caravan? The local authorities won't take kindly to finding out you might have been involved somehow in his disappearance."

I paused for a moment trying to remember the details of the message I'd sent Hannah before I set off to see Amir at the cafe.

"Just my best friend back home," I said. "I gave her Amir's name and told her to alert the U.S. Embassy in Morocco if she didn't hear from me in a week or so."

"You'd best clear out of this region at your earliest opportunity then," she said. "It will be difficult for the local police to hold you to account once you're out of the country."

"But I didn't do anything–" I began to protest.

"We're *all* implicated now. If they find Amir's dead body, they could trace any one of us to the deed. Technically, we'd all be considered accessories to the crime."

"Christ," I sighed, feeling my heart suddenly racing at the implications of what we'd done. "What the hell have I gotten myself into?"

"Don't worry," Laila said, patting my thigh reassuringly. "The desert soon buries anything that doesn't move. He'll never be found, and we'll all be long gone before anyone raises any suspicions."

"What about *Ali*?" I said. "Won't another caravan eventually find his dead body at the bottom of the well?"

"Perhaps, but with any luck it should be pretty decomposed by then. Whoever finds him will have difficulty connecting him to Amir's disappearance."

Suddenly I had a queasy feeling in the pit of my stomach, and I wrapped my arms around Laila's midsection, resting my head against her back as I peered at the never-ending hills of red sand dunes.

"How will you find your way through this wasteland all the way to Algiers?" I asked.

"The shadows of our camels will guide the way. It shows which way the sun is pointed, and all we have to do is head east and north until we reach the Mediterranean coast. From there, it should be easy to track our way to the city."

"You're a pretty smart cookie," I smiled, clutching her closely. "These girls were pretty lucky to have such a strong leader to get them out of this predicament."

"I hope they'll be happier now that they're freed from

Amir's grip," she nodded. "But I'll be sad to see some of them go. I've grown quite attached to these girls after all this time we've spent together in the desert."

Twelve hours later, the sun began to fade over the horizon and Laila stopped the group to set up camp, laying out our bedrolls amongst the circle of resting camels. Most of our food was still packed in the saddlebags and we enjoyed a peaceful dinner of rice, cooked legumes, and sweet dates. Everybody seemed much more relaxed around the campfire, chatting and giggling amongst themselves in their native arabic.

When we finished eating, we retired to our beds but soon discovered in our haste to leave the previous camp that we hadn't brought enough bedrolls and blankets for everybody to sleep on separately. Taking charge of the situation as always, Laila nestled the blankets together then we lay down as a group, not bothering to take off our robes to protect ourselves against the encroaching desert chill. It didn't take long for everyone to snuggle together for extra warmth, and before long I felt the telltale sensation of someone's fingers sliding up the bottom of my smock.

I turned around and saw Fatima smiling at me in the soft moonlight, and she leaned in to kiss me. Whether she was trying to express her gratitude for my helping to save her or she was just curious about feeling my fair skin, I couldn't be sure. But either way, I was happy to accommodate her newfound intimate interest in me. As we began to kiss more passionately, intertwining our tongues and pressing our bodies together, she pulled my robe up over my hips, caressing the outside of my thighs and my round buttocks.

But when her hand curved around to my bald pubis, she gasped and uttered something in arabic. I heard Laila reply to her in the darkness on my other side, and Fatima giggled as Laila rolled over to sandwich me between the two of them. Suddenly I had two pairs of hands caressing my body from both sides, and I moaned as they slipped their fingers between my thighs, caressing my vulva from two ends. I pulled Fatima's smock higher, feeling her fluffy bush caressing my bare mound, and I groaned in her mouth as her fingers found my pleasure spot and she began rubbing my clit in soft circular motions. But when I felt Laila's fingers press inside my slit and begin finger-fucking me from behind, I began rocking my hips, moaning more loudly.

When the rest of the girls began to realize what the three of us were up to, it didn't take long for the entire group to devolve into a moaning, slithering mass of naked bodies writhing under the thick jumble of cotton robes and woolen blankets. I pulled Fatima's dress all the way over her shoulders and squeezed her bare tits while she played with my clit and moaned into my mouth. It didn't take long for the combined action of her manipulation of my clit and Laila's caressing of my vulva to bring me to the brink of pleasure. As the two women pressed their bodies tightly against mine, I felt my orgasm overtake me and I jerked my body spastically, gushing all over the two girl's hands.

Fatima said something again to Laila, and she responded in arabic, then Fatima moved her body down closer to my midsection, apparently fascinated by my unusual bare mound and my propensity to squirt when I came. When she spread my legs apart, the other girls stopped what they were doing to peer at my dripping bald pussy glistening in the moonlight. Before I knew it, I had a clutch of pretty young girls kissing and probing every part of my body as Laila propped her head up on her elbow, smiling at me.

"Holy shit," I said to her. "You weren't kidding about how these girls like to stay entertained when the men aren't around. I think I've died and gone to *heaven!*"

"Welcome to the club, baby," Laila said, leaning in to kiss me as I felt a deluge of tongues and fingers converging on me while they sucked and nibbled on every square inch of my body. The multitude of erotic sensations soon brought me to the edge again, and I screamed in ecstasy as my whole body convulsed in another intense orgasm. Fatima suddenly pulled away from licking me while the whole group watched my pussy twitching and squirting my juices all over her face and my bare legs.

"Oh my God," I purred to Laila, after I came down from my high. "I could seriously get used to this. Are you *sure* you want to disband this group of horny young vixens?"

"Not for a couple more *days* at least," she smiled, rolling her body on top of me, grinding her dripping mound into my pliant face.

As I began to eat her pussy, the girls swarmed over top of me like a bunch of buzzing bees, rubbing their wet pussies and hairy bushes over whatever open flesh they could find on my pinned body. One of them positioned herself between my legs, pulling her pussy tight against mine and began scissoring me in a prone 'X' position while some of the other girls sucked my nipples and toes. Before we all fell asleep in a steaming pile of sweaty flesh, I must have come at least a dozen more times sucking, caressing, and fucking every one of the girls in one position or another.

As I lay on the soft desert sand surrounded by the bevy of beautiful women, I looked up toward the sky at the cloud of stars shimmering above me like a blanket of sparkling sequins. Suddenly the troubles at the previous camp seemed a hundred miles away, and I smiled at one of Amir's last comments to me. *The desert gives and takes away indeed*, I thought, as I drifted off to sleep.

8

———

For the next couple of days, we rode slowly through the desert, stopping periodically to relieve ourselves and snack on dried dates and flatbread. At night we reassembled the blankets in one large group and resumed our wild orgy under the stars until we all fell asleep, completely spent and satiated. I almost regretted seeing the dusty buildings on the edge of Algiers as we approached the city from the west, and I squeezed Laila's tummy softly to express how much I dreaded the thought of leaving her.

She parked me and the rest of the girls out of sight behind a tall dune so as not to arouse suspicion, then she led the camels three at a time into the local trading market, where she sold them at a relative bargain. It was approaching dusk by the time she returned to fetch all of us, then she took us down to the docks to arrange clandestine travel for each of the girls to return to their original towns. She gave each of them enough money to pay for the remainder of their passage, then the two of us walked along the waterfront while we talked about our next steps.

"That looked easier than I *thought* it would be," I said after all of the girls had boarded their individual ships to head home.

"These merchant seamen will transport anything for the right amount of money," she nodded.

"What about the harbormaster? How did you manage to bypass all the usual paperwork and document controls?"

"The protocols for onboarding and offboarding passengers on cargo ships are far looser on the North African coast than in Europe or America," she said, sliding her fingers and her thumb together to indicate the payment of a bribe. "Nobody seems to have a problem looking the other way as long as you grease their palms a little bit."

"How can you be sure the ships' captains will *complete* the transaction now that they've already been paid?"

"Because I promised to have them paid an *equivalent* amount once the girls safely complete their journey on the other end."

"All of this is made possible from the selling of a few *camels*?"

"Um-hm," Laila nodded. "Amir paid to take us *away* from our homes, now he's indirectly arranged to pay for them to get back."

"I'm not sure this was exactly the way he envisioned it," I frowned, trying not to think about how much he was suffering in the middle of the desert without any food or water.

"I suppose not," she chuckled. "Though I don't think *any* of this went down the way he imagined."

"So what now?" I said, peering over the Mediterranean as the sun began to set on the horizon.

"We pretend like none of this ever happened," she said. "You go back home to America, and I slip across the sea to start a new life in Spain. It shouldn't take long for us to put all of this unpleasantness behind us."

"It hasn't *all* been unpleasant," I said, grabbing her hand and pulling her into an alley to give her a long, passionate kiss. "I'll have far more *happy* memories to hold onto than this one unfortunate affair."

"Mmm," she nodded, pressing her body up tightly against me.

"Well isn't *this* a happy little reunion," a familiar man's voice suddenly cackled from the shadows.

Laila and I swung around to see Amir blocking the exit to the alley, brandishing his glinty curved knife.

"I knew the two of you were up to no good the moment I saw you ogling each other during the belly dance performance in my tent. And now it's time for the lot of you to be held to account for your transgressions. Right after you tell me what you've done with the other girls."

I stared at Amir with my mouth agape in a mix of shock and confusion.

"How—"

"Did I manage to get all this way on foot?" he said. "Your first mistake was leaving me with all the livestock. Their milk and meat can sustain a man for a long time in the desert. Plus, I was lucky enough to catch another passing caravan after a couple of days. If you two hadn't dawdled taking your time crossing the desert, you might have made a clean getaway by now." He paused, running his eyes up and down our bodies. "Of course, I didn't have any *other* distractions encouraging me to pause for a little entertainment in the evenings."

"So I suppose you've alerted the elders by now and arranged for us to be taken before the council to be properly punished?" Laila said, stepping in front of me and placing her arm around me protectively.

"In due course," he said. "First I needed to *find* you before you slipped away. I'm afraid your fate, along with the rest of my little harem, has already been sealed, Laila." Then he turned toward me, clucking his tongue. "As for my pretty Western friend, I'm sure we can find a dark prison somewhere in the bowels of this medieval city to let her rot away the rest of her miserable life."

Amir lurched forward, placing the knife under Laila's neck.

"Now *tell* me where the rest of the girls are!" he sneered.

Suddenly, Laila reared back, kicking Amir as hard as she could between his legs and he hunched over, dropping the knife onto the ground. She quickly picked it up and before he could regain his composure, she sliced it across the front of his neck in one quick and silent motion. He clutched his throat, looking at us with wild eyes, then he fell to his knees, collapsing onto the cobblestone pavement. As a thick pool of blood seeped out of his jugular vein onto the darkened stones, the life slowly drained out of his eyes, and he suddenly became still.

"Holy *fuck*, Laila," I gasped. "You *killed* him!"

"It was either him or us," she said nonchalantly. "He got what was coming to him."

"What the hell do we do now?" I said, looking around frantically to see if anyone else had witnessed the scene. "We can't just *leave* him here. He can be traced back to us."

Laila paused for a moment as she peered around the wharf to get her bearings, then she nodded toward a nearby dock.

"We'll have to drag him to the edge of the jetty and dump him into the water. There's no one around and it's dark enough for us to dispose of the body. Grab a leg and help me pull him toward the pier."

I shook my head, hardly believing how fast our plan had unraveled and wondering what would happen if anyone saw us. But I knew Laila was right. Between the front desk attendant at my hotel in Morocco and my email trail to Hannah, there was more than enough circumstantial evidence to connect me to Amir's disappearance. The best chance for both of us to get away before the police caught wind of any malfeasance was to dispose of the body and exit as quickly as possible.

We each grabbed one of Amir's legs and after checking to make sure the coast was clear, we carefully dragged his body the thirty feet or so across the narrow roadway lining the wharf and dropped his lifeless body into the murky water at the edge of the pier. We watched his body slowly sink into the deep water, then we ducked into another alley to decide what to do next.

"So what do we do now?" I said, shivering from a combination of shock and the encroaching chill.

"You've still got your travel bag and papers," she said, nodding toward my clutch case. "You need to get changed back into your Western clothes as soon as possible and catch the earliest flight out of the country. With any luck, you'll be long gone before anyone finds any evidence of foul play. I'll pay for safe passage to the continent and try to slip into Spain undetected. Right now, we both have to get the hell out of here."

"Okay," I said, wrapping my arms around my body to keep myself from shaking. "But will I ever see you again? I hate leaving you this way..."

"It's best we make a clean break," she said, pulling me close against her breast. "We don't want anyone connecting us together after this. You'll be fine. I'll think of you when-ever I'm sleeping alone under my woolen blanket."

I paused for a moment, darting my eyes across her pretty face. I hated the idea of leaving so abruptly, but I knew we didn't have any other choice. I opened my travel bag and scribbled my address on a piece of paper.

"This is my address back home in America," I said, handing her the paper. "Just do me one favor. Write me once you get situated in Spain and send me your address. It'll be safe to see you again once this all settles down. I'd love to be able to stay in touch."

"Okay," Laila said, folding the paper and tucking it away into her robe. "But you need to go now. I want you to catch the earliest flight out in the morning. I'll contact you once I get settled."

She leaned in towards me, clasping the sides of my head with both hands.

"This has been the most amazing adventure of my life," she said. "I'll never forget these few days we've shared together, my beautiful sweet, American girl. Safe travels, my love. We'll talk again soon."

Then she turned and walked briskly down the wharf into the inky darkness without looking back. I watched her robes billowing in the cool evening breeze until she disap-peared in the mist, then I changed out of my thawb in the darkness of the alley and put my Western clothes back on, hailing a cab to the airport. I was lucky enough to catch the seven a.m. flight to Paris with a connecting flight to Chicago later that day. As my jet lifted off the runway and turned north over the Mediterranean Sea, I peered down at the wide expanse of sparking blue waves, smiling at how it reminded me of the golden sand ripples in the desert.

After I got home, a few months passed without hearing from Laila, and I began to fear that she might not have made it out of the North Africa. But when I received an airmail letter postmarked Seville, Spain, I tore it open and read the contents breathlessly.

Jade,

I hope this letter finds you well and fully recovered from our little desert adventure. I've thought of you often since we departed so suddenly in Algiers and miss having your smooth, supple body snuggling up next to me. You may be happy to know that I've grown quite accustomed to your Western-style grooming habits and I always think of you whenever I touch myself on dark, lonely nights. If ever you find the time to come visit me, I've enclosed my new address below.

Love always, Laila

Oh my God, I exhaled, happy to hear that she'd made it out safely. And the fact that she still had fond memories of our time together and even thought of me whenever she touched herself intimately made my heart dance and my panties moisten. As I sat in my chair rereading her letter over and over again and smelling the delicate scent of jasmine and lemongrass infused in the paper, my fingers trailed a path down between my thighs as I separated my legs slowly.

Maybe this won't be the end of my arabian adventure after all, I smiled to myself.

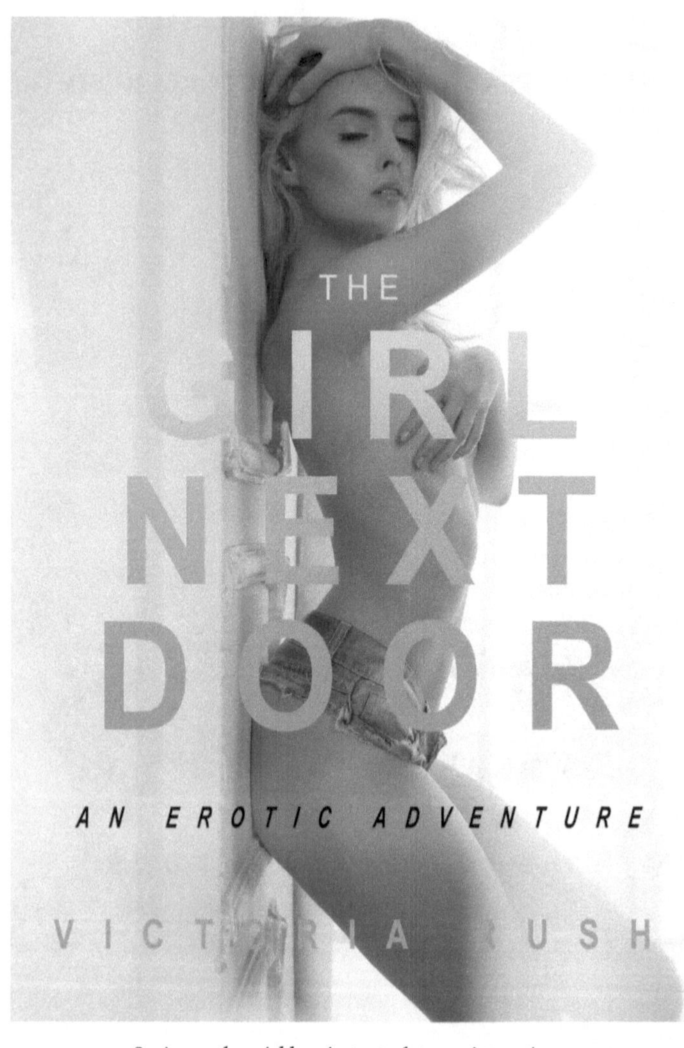

Spying on the neighbors just got a lot more interesting...

Everything's sexier in the dark

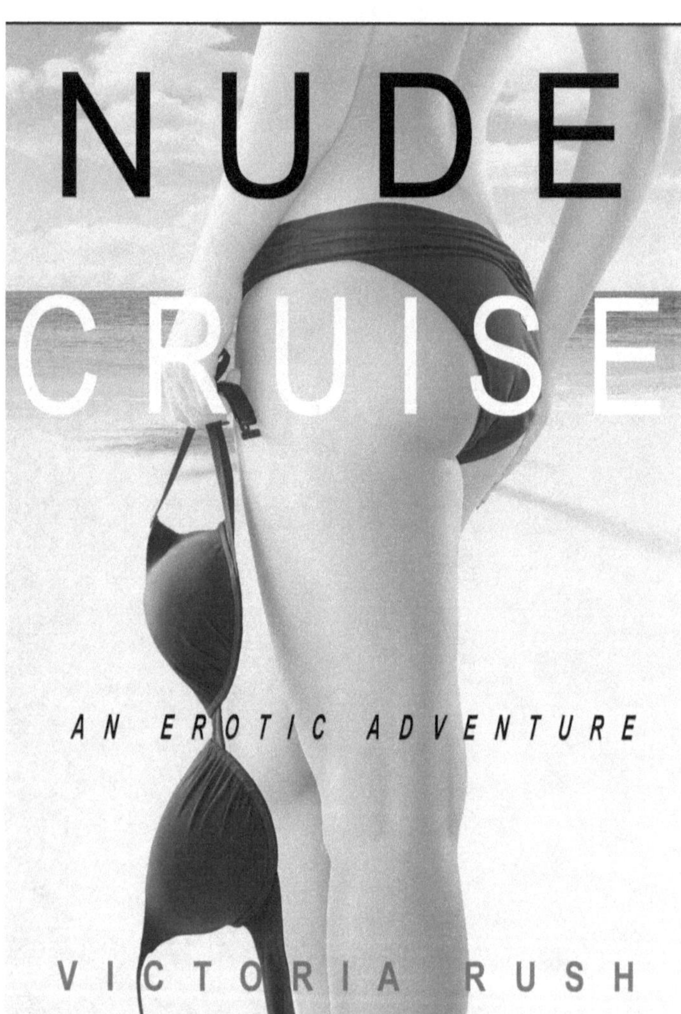

Some people get wet on a cruise for different reasons...

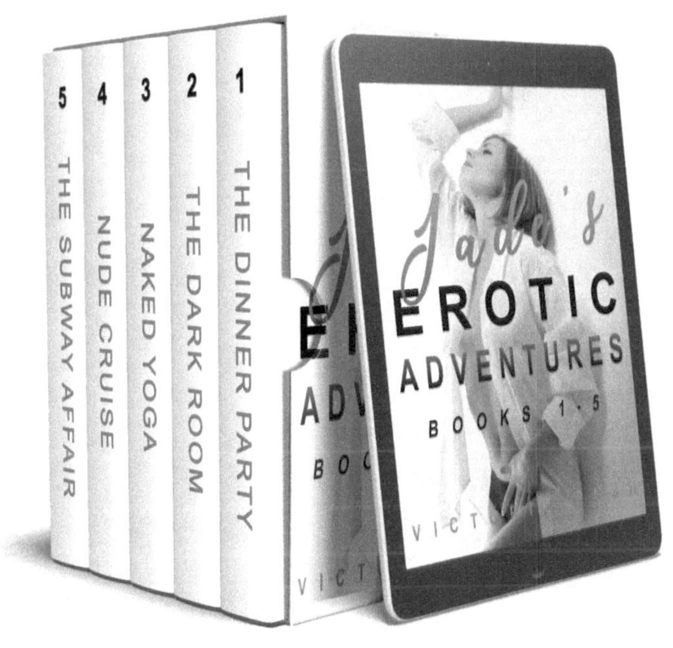

Books 1 -5 in the bestselling erotica series - 60% off

THE DARE - PREVIEW
CHAPTER 3

"Okay, so now that I'm committed, tell me where you had in mind for this little experiment."

"Actually," Hannah said, "I have a *series* of places in mind, each one more challenging than the one before."

"But I thought you said this was a one-off proposition?"

"I said nothing of the sort. I only said that if you won, I'd pay for the flights to Bora Bora. If you want me to cover the cost of hotels, food, and all the other incidentals, you'll have to pass progressively tougher tests. We don't want to make this *too* easy for you, do we?"

I crossed my arms and huffed, putting on my best pouty face.

"It hardly seems fair," I said. "But I'm still game. Besides, either one of us can pull out at any time to lock in our gains, right?"

"I suppose so," Hannah shrugged. "But what would be the fun in that? Something tells me once you've tried the first experiment, you won't want to stop. I think you're going to find this whole thing quite titillating and exciting. This will be the most fun either one of us has had in a long time."

I pushed the rest of my half-eaten salmon dish to the side, suddenly no longer interested in eating.

"Okay, lay it on me then. Where are you planning to take me for the first test?

Hannah gulped down the rest of her margarita then peered at me with a lopsided grin.

"Church. More specifically, a *Catholic* church. You haven't been in quite a while, have you? This will be your chance to repent and atone for all your sins."

"It's not like I've broken any commandments or anything–"

"The Catholic Church still considers sex outside of marriage a mortal sin. So technically, you've been doing a ton of sinning since your marriage ended."

"Well I haven't been a practicing Catholic for ages," I snorted. "So my conscience is clear. This'll be a cakewalk. All I have to do is sit quietly in my pew, right?"

"Yes, but it'll be a *front-row* pew, in full view of the priest who'll be delivering the sermon."

"Okay, but I'll be fully clothed, right? It's not like there'll be anything for him to see..."

"Not if you can keep your composure and don't cum all over the floor," Hannah said, cocking her head playfully.

"I don't think I'll have any difficulty keeping my dick in my pants, in a manner of speaking. But you raise a good point. You can't expect me not to get a little wet while you're stimulating me. What will I be allowed to wear?"

"I assume you'll dress appropriately, wearing your Sunday best. A mid-length skirt and button-up blouse should do the trick. You should be able to hide a few dribbles that way, right?"

"I suppose so, but how will we muffle the sound of the vibrator buzzing inside my panties? There's likely to be other people sitting around me in adjacent pews..."

"Never fear," Hannah smiled, reaching into her purse and pulling out a U-shaped silicone sex toy. "I've been talking with our friend at the local Babeland store. She's given me the latest prototype of the We-Vibe vibrator to test." She held up a smaller device with two control buttons and a flywheel. "Complete with a Bluetooth remote control. And the best thing is that it's whisper-quiet.

"Here," she said, handing me the flexible device. "See for yourself."

She tapped one of the buttons on the remote and the thick side of the contraption began buzzing softly in my hand.

"Okay," I nodded, looking around me to see if any other restaurant patrons were distracted by the gentle hum of the object. "It's *quiet* enough, but which end goes inside?"

"The bulbous end is a natural G-spot stimulator. You place the flatter end against your clit, then pull the thing up tight against your vulva to keep it snugly in place."

I suddenly became mindful of the wetness permeating my panties as I imagined the device vibrating inside me, surrounded by a bunch of oblivious bystanders.

"Can I give it a try here, like we did last time?" I grinned.

"No way," Hannah said, pulling the toy out of my hands. "There'll be no trial runs for this or any future tests. You'll just have to wait until we get to the church."

"And where will *you* be sitting while this is all going down?" I said.

"Right next to you, of course. I'll want a front-row seat to watch all the action."

On Sunday morning, Hannah picked me up and drove me the two miles to our local church. The entire time I squirmed in my seat trying to imagine what it would be like having a vibrator buzzing inside me in the quiet chapel. When we got to the church parking lot, she pulled into a sheltered space then plucked the blue vibrator out of her purse and handed it to me, resting her arm on the seat cushion expectantly.

"*What?*" I said. "You don't trust me to put it in privately?"

"Not really," she smirked. "For all I know, you might pull on some adult diapers under your skirt to hide any unintended releases. Here," she said, handing me a plastic vial. "I brought some lube to make it go in easier."

"I don't need any," I said, pulling the vibrator out of her hands and placing it under my skirt. "I'm already plenty worked up thinking about this scenario."

"I hope you're wearing panties under that skirt," Hannah said, watching me shift my weight as I placed the device against my vulva. "We wouldn't want it popping out at an inopportune moment."

"I'll just have to leave that up to your imagination," I sneered, lifting my skirt halfway up my thigh. "Unless you need to inspect the goods to make sure I'm not cheating."

"I trust you," Hannah smiled, opening her car door. "Something tells me you're looking forward to this just as much as I am."

As we approached the entrance to the church, I noticed a familiar figure standing at the top of the steps greeting the incoming parishioners, and he made eye contact with me when Hannah and I approached the landing.

"Jade!" Father Fife said, holding out his hands to me. "I haven't seen you in such a long time. It's so good to have you join us again."

"I'm sorry, Father," I said, placing my sweaty hand between his. "I've been a little distracted lately..."

"Life has a habit of getting in the way of the important things," he said. "We're just glad to have you whenever you can find time." He turned to Hannah, raising his eyebrows in curiosity. "And who's this lovely lady you've brought with you to attend our service today?"

"This is Hannah," I said, motioning toward my friend. "I thought I'd bring her along for moral support."

"Happy to have you, Hannah," Father Fife said, clasping Hannah's hands warmly. "The Lord knows we all need moral support wherever we can find it."

Hannah nodded politely, then the two of us walked through the entrance doors where I dipped my hand into the bowl of holy water and crossed my chest before continuing on toward the front of the chapel.

"*Jesus,*" Hannah whispered, peering around the imposing shrine. "Is it just me, or did that feel a little creepy? All that talk about *having* us and that prolonged hand-holding. Hasn't he been paying any attention to the me-too movement?"

"I'm not sure any of that applies to men of the *cloth,*" I chuckled. "But you better be careful about using the Lord's name like that around here. If anybody overhears you, you're liable to be burned at the stake."

The two of us stepped lively down the main aisle and finding a free spot in the front row, we took our seats flanked by two elderly couples. It was hard to imagine how Hannah would be able to use the remote-control device sandwiched so closely between other parishioners, and I crossed my legs, thankful for the brief respite. When everyone had filed into the chapel and the bell signaled the start of the service, a hush fell over the chamber and we all stood up as Father Fife walked onto the pulpit in his flowing robes.

"In the name of the Father, and of the Son, and of the Holy Spirit," he intoned solemnly.

"Amen," the congregation murmured in unison.

"The Lord be with you," he said.

"And with your spirit," the couples beside me retorted.

What the hell have I gotten myself into? I thought, feeling the flexible vibrator pressing against the inside of my closed legs. I didn't consider myself a terribly religious person, but being in this holy place surrounded by all the familiar rituals brought back all the old memories from my parents about the consequences of sinful behavior. *Surely getting secretly stimulated by a sex toy in the house of God will send me straight to hell.*

This was the point in the church service where everybody was supposed to take a moment to make a penitential act. While I listened to the other parishioners around me making their supplications, my knees began shaking as I made my own silent prayer for forgiveness.

"May Almighty God have mercy on us all," the priest said. "Forgive us our sins, and bring us to everlasting life."

"Amen," I joined in the congregation's response.

"Let us pray," Father Fife said, bowing his head.

As we closed our eyes and he began his opening prayer, Hannah nudged me with her knee and my mind raced with images of the pastor scornfully looking down at us while we played our blasphemous game. I peered up as he flapped his Bible closed, and caught him glancing in my direction.

"Through our Lord Jesus Christ, your Son," he said. "Who lives and reigns with you in the unity of the Holy Spirit, one God forever and ever."

"Amen," I said aloud, hoping he'd see me behaving like a good Catholic girl and turn his attention elsewhere.

He motioned for everyone to sit down and I was glad to get off my shaky feet onto the relative safety of the wooden pew.

"Good morning, ladies and gentlemen," he began his homily. "Today, I would like to talk with you about *morality*. Specifically, about the decaying state of society's morals in today's world. All around us we are surrounded by prurient symbols of modern decadence. First it was in the form of the printed word, then motion pictures, then the ubiquitous internet. It seems everywhere we turn, we are bombarded with profane and sacrilegious images."

I felt my heart pounding in my chest, like he was singling me out personally for my not-so-infrequent porn surfing.

"We seem to have forgotten," he railed, "the Lord's commandment that we shall not covet thy neighbor's wife. This admonition can be taken in its broadest context. Not only have many of you forsaken the sacred institution of marriage, but the egregious and widespread popularity of obscene *pornography* belies our unbridled lust and depravity. God slew Onan for spilling his seed, and so He will strike all others who practice self-abuse."

Hannah nudged her knee against mine, suddenly

reminding me why we were here. I was glad that she hadn't yet had the opportunity to take out her remote-control device, and I prayed that we'd be able to get through most of the service without her rudely interrupting it. I'd already begun to regret agreeing to this little venture, and I hoped that somehow we'd be able to bypass this first phase in her experiment.

"I'd like you to pick up your Bibles," Father Fife said, interrupting my thoughts. "And turn to Mark, Chapter 7, Verse 20."

Hannah and I reached down to pick up the bibles lying on the seat beside each of us, and we flipped to the indicated section.

"Read this passage with me, my friends," Father Fife instructed. "What comes *out* of a person is what defiles him," he enunciated, while the congregation quietly murmured along.

As I began to recite the passage along with him, I saw Hannah reach into her side pocket and place her closed hand between the book binding.

"For from within come evil thoughts," I continued reading as I peered out of the corner of my eye to see what she was up to.

"Sexual immorality, adultery, coveting, wickedness..." we read in unison.

Suddenly, I felt the interior end of the vibrator begin to tremble inside me and I stuttered, trying to finish the passage.

"Deceit...sensuality...envy..." I stammered, trying to catch my breath as I followed along. Hearing my labored recital, Hannah turned her head in my direction, acknowledging my silent suffering. She knew exactly what I was feeling and how difficult it was for me to remain composed as I read the script.

"All these evil things...come from *within*," I gulped as I began to feel the pleasure spread across my pelvic region. "And they defile a person."

"Consider these words carefully," the priest said, surveying my hunched-over posture. "For the Lord does not abide salacious thoughts and behavior. If you want passage into His Kingdom, you must be as pure and righteous as He."

He paused for a moment to let the message sink in, then he motioned with his two hands for us to be seated. I was grateful for the rest, and I froze upright in my chair trying to ignore the movement of the possessed instrument inside me.

"Let us consider for a moment *another* one of God's ten commandments," Father Fife continued. "Thou shall not commit *adultery*. The Lord made Eve from the flesh of Adam, and in so doing signified that forever more man shall be united to his wife as one..."

As Father Fife ramped up the intensity of his gayphobic critique, so did Hannah, furtively adjusting the flywheel on the remote-control device nestled under her palm in her lap. As she slowly increased the speed of the vibrations emanating inside my pussy, I squirmed on the bench, trying to restrain my rising passion.

"By rejecting the sanctity of marriage," Father Fife continued, glancing distractedly in my direction, "you have all *sinned*. In the book of Deuteronomy, we saw that God ordered adulterers be stoned to death. For your indiscriminate behavior, so shall the Lord indiscriminately smite thee."

Jesus, I thought. If that's what awaits a sinner for

cheating on their spouse, I wonder what happens to someone who self-abuses herself while sitting for Sunday Service in a house of God. *Surely I'll burn in hell for this act of sacrilege.*

Just when I thought I was beginning to get control over the delicious sensations stimulating my insides, Father Fife instructed us to stand once again and recite another passage from the Bible.

"Please stand now and read Peter 1:16 with me," he said.

Everyone stood and dutifully flipped to the relevant section of the scriptures. This time it was even harder for me to stand motionless, as my knees fluttered unsteadily from the pleasurable sensations radiating inside me.

"It is written..." I tried to read along. "That you shall be holy, for I am holy."

I saw Hannah's hands moving once again inside her prayer book, and suddenly I felt the *other* end of the U-shaped vibrator buzzing against my clit.

"And now Galatians 5:16," Father Fife instructed, barely giving me a chance to recover.

I flipped to the new citation and gasped for breath as my legs wobbled beneath me.

"But I say," I panted unsteadily. "Walk by the Spirit, and you will not gratify the desires of the flesh."

"So it is written," Father Fife said, closing his Bible. "Be righteous as the Lord, and you shall join him in Heaven for everlasting days. And now," he said, magnifying my torture. "I would like us to sing together one of my favorite hymns celebrating His blessing, *Amazing Grace*. Please pick up your hymn books and turn to page forty-three."

"Amazing grace, how sweet the sound," the priest began to sing as the entire congregation joined him in harmony.

"That saved a wretch like me," I sang along, trying to

ignore the message that seemed targeted directly at me. As I tried to hold the melody, Hannah cupped the remote-control device in her hand and turned the flywheel to its maximum setting.

"I once was lost, but now am found," I hyperventilated, pressing my legs together as hard as I could to stifle the rising passion that threatened to overtake me.

"Was blind, but now I see," I squealed, singing the last word decidedly off-pitch as Father Fife turned to see my entire body shaking as I belted the famous hymn.

By the time I'd finished the song, I'd somehow managed to keep it together and fight off the cresting passion that had threatened to put me over the edge. When we finally sat back down, Hannah mercifully turned the vibrator off, and I spread my hands over my ruffled skirt to signal that I'd managed to keep myself composed.

When the service was over and we walked up the aisle behind the rest of the assembly to exit the church, I couldn't wait to get out of the building to wash myself off, figuratively and literally. I was glad that we were at the back of the crowd so nobody could see the back of my skirt. I wasn't sure if my leaking pussy had left a stain, but I sure as hell didn't want one of the parishioners pointing it out. When we finally exited the entrance doors, Father Fife turned to the two of us and smiled.

"I noticed you seemed a little more passionate than usual reciting today's passages, Jade" he said to me.

"Yes, Father," I said, shaking his hand unsteadily. "I felt truly embodied by the spirit."

"And *you*, Hannah," he nodded. "Did you enjoy today's service also?"

"Oh yes," she said. "It was the most moving sermon I've attended in a long time."

"I hope you'll both come again," Father Fife said to the two of us.

"I'm sure we *will*, Father," Hannah smiled as we continued down the steps.

Like the second we get back home, I thought to myself, dying to tear off my clothes and squirt all over Hannah's face while she ate out my still-dripping pussy.

READ MORE...

ABOUT THE AUTHOR

If you would like to receive notification of new book(s) in Jade's Erotic Adventures, follow me at http://bookbub.com/authors/victoria-rush.

If you have a moment, please post a brief review on my Amazon book page at viewbook.at/theharem . Even just a couple of sentences will help other readers find and enjoy this book as much as you hopefully did.

Follow, share, like, and comment at:

www.facebook.com/authorvictoriarush
www.pinterest.com/authorvictoriarush
www.twitter.com/authorvictoriarush
authorvictoriarush@outlook.com

Hope to see you again soon!